A Simple Tale of Sugar and Shadows

THE SIMPLE TALES BOOKS

KAMI KING LARSEN

"For he would be thinking of love
        Till the stars had run away
        And the shadows eaten the moon."

-W.B. Yeats

Please be advised, this is meant to be a light and cozy read. However, there are references to death of a parent, abduction, emotional manipulation, mild violence, as well as witchcraft, creepy carousels, heartbreak, and overconsumption of sweets. Enjoy!

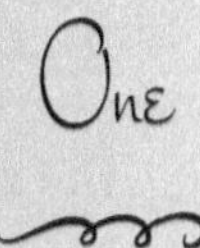

One

The scent of burnt sugar and subtle magic filled his nose. Darkness's expression changed only marginally—from indifference to slight curiosity and back again—as he took in the dancing lights and bubbles of laughter. Ordinarily, he would have found the combination of magic and confections little more than nostalgic. He'd spent endless nights separating himself from anything more. But over the proceeding weeks, it had been growing stronger in the air, and he was no longer stalwart enough to ignore it. He was finally giving in to the welcome comfort of the mix.

The carnival itself wasn't altogether unexpected. At any given time, a handful of touring groups were traipsing across the countryside in unending loops. Some traveled by train, others by wagon alone. None had yet adopted the reeking new petrol-powered trucks. No matter how they traveled, it had become habit for him to ignore the lights and the merriment, the music and the joy.

This time, however, had been different. Maybe it was the trace of magic that made him take note. The competing carnivals were mundane things after all. But the moment he'd scented it on the wind, it put him in mind of another time. One he returned to only in the darkest of his dreams.

The locals up and down the coast would embrace the frivolity, the distraction of it all—even if it cost them in coins better spent on things less trivial. And who was he to judge? By most estimations, Darkness—also known by a few as Dub —did one questionable thing after another.

With nothing to anchor him, he'd let himself detach and float along. His brothers didn't suffer a similar fate, content as they were to be what they were made to be.

The carnival crew had done a worthy job of announcing themselves without giving it all away. The tents on the outward side of the barrier looked like the sort you'd find at any market up and down the coast. The standard fare was being sold from stalls of simple canvas and rolling wooden carts. Roasted ears of sweet corn drizzled with honey, steaming hand pies of mutton and potato, stalls brimming with flower crowns and wands braided with bright silk ribbons. Even a worn-down wagon laden with tapped kegs of ale and other bitter spirits.

The villagers here would be happy to drop a few coins on any number of minor treats before they ventured deeper into the heart of the carnival. It was there that promises of thrills awaited.

The scent of sugar and the waves of magic were easy to trace from farther down the coast. He'd been in Feyport with his mother the days past and had been itching for any excuse to set out on his own for a spell. He'd become *unsettled* there and that just wouldn't do.

Darkness wasn't sure what to make of that village's new name—Feyport. For ages he'd known it as one thing or another, and while he had no wish to go back to the dark times when it was just as nameless as so many other towns and road-side spots, he found the chosen moniker disquieting. Names were important. Names meant something. He himself had more than one. But Feyport seemed just a bit too direct. *A bit too on the button.* He hoped the carnival would pass it by on this loop of the circuit.

The clash of the fey-filled village and this unusual carnival felt inevitable however. It was a shame really. If its denizens truly wanted thrills and excitement, all they need do was look about them. It was all right under their noses, just as the name stated.

For those with average ordinary lives, the carnival offered safety dressed up as thrills. It offered young couples looking to clasp each other tight a reason to do so. It offered groups of men the chance to prove their strength or glimpse a flash of skin outside the confines of a marriage bed. It offered young women danger dressed up in a safe story to later share with their friends. And of course, the life's blood of carnivals—the families—it offered naïve parents a place to let their children roam free. It offered these things, but Darkness didn't have an average ordinary life, and he knew better than to believe the pretty lie.

The scent of magic meant danger lurked here just as surely as he did.

One would have thought folks would sense the tendrils of otherness simmering below the surface façade. For this was no ordinary fair, no cozy carnival. He could feel it in his marrow.

But people see what they are willing to see. Darkness knew that as much as anyone.

He wasn't one to hope for much, but he held out a strange sort of hope for Feyport. Maybe the unordinary carnival would skip the seaside village his mother had such a fondness for. Maybe whoever had magic enough to maintain the show as it traveled up and down the countryside would know the residents there didn't need their trickery. Maybe he could slip in tonight, see what he needed to see, and slip right out again.

After all, the carnival folk weren't the only ones who knew a trick or two. Maybe no one, save himself, would be wise to his jaunt.

A long line had formed on the outskirts of the tents, and though he could have bled into the shadows and bypassed it entirely, Darkness took his place at the end. Those around him gave him a wide berth—not necessarily knowing who or what he was, but sensing the danger all the same.

On the surface, the magic of the place was beautiful in its simplicity—something his mother would enjoy. It bent with the shadows and bled into the night—something *he* enjoyed. The seemingly ordinary tents with their seemingly ordinary wares were each kissed with the faintest blush of fey magic. If one wasn't looking for it, they would miss it.

But the man known by some as Dub and many others as Darkness *was* looking, and he didn't miss a drop.

What was more, this magic didn't remain simple and beautiful. It ran deeper than the surface charms. The closer he snaked along in the line, the stronger the undercurrent became. It was dark and it was mean and it had no business pretending otherwise.

As he moved farther up the queue, he studied the outer edges—a thin rope pulled between posts, more a suggestion of a barrier than an actual obstruction. The music from within the rope grew marginally less muted, and he struggled to decipher if it was purposeful or some minor fault in the magic.

He wondered who had the running of the carnival. It seemed quite similar to *her* carnival, but that had been a very *very* long time ago. Surely it was just happenchance. Or more likely yet, his mind was telling him it was similar when surely it was far more modern and not the same at all.

Darkness blinked and cleared his mind. Thinking about *her* would do little but bring him sorrow.

As the music solidified, the three young women in front of

him took the melody as a cue to begin dancing. They were subtle at first. Just a sweep of the arms or a step to the side. The barest sway of a hip. But as they approached the entrance, their movements grew less guarded. They held hands and laughed as if not a care could touch them. The tallest of the three had golden hair that fell loose to her shoulders. She was pretty in a conventional way, and Darkness imagined she was used to having eyes on her. As one of the other girls twirled her around, her mouth popped open in a small "O" at the sight of him. In a flash, the "O" transformed into a full and presumptuous grin. She tugged her arms free from her friends and stepped closer to him. Darkness had no trouble keeping his expression placid and disinterested as her tongue darted out and licked at her lower lip.

"Hello." He imagined she thought her breathy voice intriguing. It was not. "I knew coming here tonight would be worth the time and the coins."

One of her friends giggled, but as the darkness around them grew deeper, the laughter died on her lips. She took a nervous step backward. The brazen one, transfixed as she was, didn't seem to notice.

Darkness sighed, bored of the games people played when they had no idea of the rules. She clearly had not an inkling of who—or better, what—he was. If she did, she would have been much less enamored by his striking face.

He knew what many saw when they took him in. Dark hair and darker eyes and darkest of all an expression that brought women and men alike to their knees. Only his alabaster skin provided any contrast in his visage. Truly, his mother had been an artisan in his making, but she'd been even more skilled with what lay below his surface.

"The queue moves on, lovie"—he nodded behind her to the snake of people between them and the tent serving as gateway to the carnival—"and so must you."

The woman started as if slapped, her cheeks flushing ever so slightly, unaccustomed to being so quickly dismissed. The second of her companions, a petite plain thing, snorted a laugh that couldn't be concealed by the hand she pressed to her mouth. Her dress was simple, but Darkness sensed the woman herself was not. He raised a brow, and she looked down at her toes.

The queue continued to move, the gap widening as the trio stood rooted to the spot, unsure what to make of the man behind them. Perhaps the tall one wished for adventure, but Darkness felt her companions were merely too wary to turn their backs on him. Either way, the dallying grated along his skin.

"The queue, ladies." His expression spoke louder than his quiet words. The trio turned and hastened forward. Every so often one of them would shoot a furtive look over their shoulder.

Darkness did well to stay a good distance back.

If his brothers had been in attendance, it would have been so much worse. Some might have thought the idea of Dain and Dother—Violence and Evil—at the carnival ridiculous. But Darkness knew better. He knew *them*. It wouldn't be ridiculous at all. It would be calamitous.

A handful of minutes passed, and the line made its slow progression forward. Darkness might have simply melted into the shadows only to reappear inside the grounds, but his impatience needed to be tempered. Self-control hadn't always been his strong suit, and it had cost him dearly. He'd vowed long ago he would temper himself and give none a reason to take his destiny from him again.

And so, like the nitwits before him, and the long serpentine of people to his back, he shuffled slowly forward until he came to a small wooden structure occupied by a smiling young woman in striped tights, a tiny violet bowler, and matching ruched bustle. Wordlessly, he handed her a coin, and in return she gave him a crisp red ticket.

It took only a glance at the ornate script for his heart to stutter.

"Elwell & Sons."

The name was printed with such flourish.

How long since he'd seen the eponym? Decades? A century? Longer. It had been in his youth so very long ago. And in his dreams each night since.

He blinked and looked again.

Not Elwell.

Colger. Colger & Sons.

It was otherwise so similar. The same swirling script, inky black against the same muted shade of red.

An easy mistake to make.

"Means little." Darkness muttered the words as his feet pushed him closer to the raucous noise of the carnival proper.

Past the wooden ticket stall the line curved toward a dust-covered tent. It appeared just large enough to house a ticket taker. The night was full of flickering candles and glowing lamps. Darkness pulled the shadows tighter, dimming the space around him.

The women in front of him were all giggles and excitement, their earlier unease forgotten. The mousy one bounced up and down on her toes as if she'd been waiting for this evening all her life. And who knew? Perhaps she had. They approached the tent—its diminutive size merely an illusion—then all three women entered through a flap in the canvas. Laughter bubbled up and then hushed as the flap dropped shut.

A moment later a voice from within barked for the next patron to enter.

Darkness obliged.

The space was indeed much larger than it had appeared

from the outside. He had plenty of room to stand his full height and more than enough space between him and the showman collecting the stubs.

The ticket taker was an older man with a sharp nose and wispy whiskers covering a chin gone soft with age and a life spent on the road. A puckered scar tugged one corner of his mouth down in a perpetual frown to match the furrow dividing his brow. Not friendly this one. All business. Darkness could relate.

The ticket taker's gaze was shrewd as he took in the man entering his tent. A knowing flashed through his cloudy eyes, but he lifted his chin all the same, unwilling to cower. Still, it was hard to miss the tremor in his hand as he reached for the stub in Darkness's hand.

Darkness winked as he handed it over. "As I hear it, there are wonders awaiting."

The man's left eye twitched.

"Contortionist and the like?"

The man said nothing.

It wasn't a show he was after, but something far subtler and much much sweeter. There was no need to share this with the ticket man.

He held out his hand as the torn stub was given back. Darkness glanced at the paper and tucked it in his vest pocket.

The showman snorted, a mix of false bravado, disgust, and downright terror on his face. "The show ends at midnight. Make sure you're out by then." He jerked his head toward the wall opposite and Darkness tipped his head as he grabbed the flap. Pushing the heavy material back and dragging his gloom along with him, he exited into the rollicking night.

The music slammed into him with the force of its vitality. It was a thing just as much felt as heard, and Darkness relished in each thumping beat and calliope melody. They should have been clashing, but the various tunes from different areas of the carnival came together in a wondrous cacophony.

If he had been a different man, he might have smiled as the sound hit him. There had been a time when he had all but lived for similar nights. But those nights were many moons past. Even had it been yesterday, he would still have found it wondrous. Not wondrous enough to elicit a smile, but that had nothing to do with this particular carnival and everything to do with Darkness himself. This carnival was nothing short of amazing, even for a man who had seen his share of wonders.

It wasn't just the music, carnal and sweet—a living thing which seemed to drag more than one visitor off in directions they didn't choose for themselves. It was the tiny floating lights shimmering in every direction, their incandescence burning into his eyes so even as he closed his lids, the dots remained and blossomed. It was the heady aroma of cooking meat and the musky smell of sweat. Of caramel and salt, marshmallow and popping corn. It was the faint prickles of magic dancing along his skin and the taste of lust and fear and stunning disbelief that flavored each breath he took.

Yes, it was wondrous. But he was who he was. Not as he had been. Time and circumstances and life had molded him. As wondrous as he found the atmosphere, he had a task to complete. Smiling wasn't required.

The task was simple. Explore the setting. Let his mind recall for just a handful of hours what it would. Then bottle it all back up and shelve it safely away once more. Remind himself who he was and be done with it.

"Stunning, Mother." Darkness shook his head as he continued to take it all in. It was much the same as he remembered yet it was also so much more.

In the past handful of years, there had been a noticeable resurgence of the fey magic he remembered from his youth, but *this*? This carnival was teeming with magic. Far more than he ever would have expected to find centered in one place. The ringmaster—or ringmasters more like—must have been either terribly powerful or terribly stupid to waste such magic on sideshows and frivolities. It should have been spent solely in the big top where it could be hidden and contained. A draw for the crowds to cap off the night.

Unless. . .

All thoughts of the memories which had originally drawn him there were gone. Darkness scanned the area again—this time looking as his mother, the witch Carman, would look. A deep well of magic had to be somewhere close. He simply needed to open his senses and find it. He'd been drawn there by memories but, upon feeling that sooty pool of arcane magic, found that he had work to do. Better then to remember now who he was and not after some pathetic stroll through his past.

"Where to start. Where to start." His gaze bounced from one stall to the next. From tent to pristine tent. Fortune tellers, oddities, and petting menageries were interspersed with tents offering thrills and scares. There were kissing booths and calliopes. A series of stalls to test one's luck and more to test one's strength. A maze of dark crystal mirrors and a large brocade big top, the fabric of which was almost too rich to be real. A rickety coaster ride and next to it. . .

His heart skipped a beat and he stifled a choked breath.

A confectionary wagon.

Its design wasn't in step with the current style but rather was nearly identical to his memory. But truly, after months, years, decades. . . It had to be another coincidence. Just someone's idea of nostalgic good fun. Pink and white and striped and cozy.

Coincidence or no, it didn't matter. Just that fast, the draw was back. He was being tested and he was failing miserably.

His memories resurfaced. His pain again blossomed. His reason for following the scent of the magic and the scent of the memories warred with his newfound quest to uncover the source of the strangely powerful enchantment.

He could do both. He was Darkness after all.

Almost of their own accord, his feet started in the direction of the sweet-laden cart. He passed rows of stalls designed to separate folks from their coin in a ridiculous hope of winning a useless potion or cleverly crafted false wings. Darkness tried not to notice, but the part of him that was his mother's son cataloged each tiny detail and cleverly crafted glamour as he moved through the crowd.

The closer he got to the confectionary, the closer he drew to the big top. The massive tent oozed a magic that wasn't precisely menacing, but it also wasn't natural. Or, at least, he had thought that was where it stemmed from. Now he was no longer certain. It wouldn't be easily pinpointed, and that irritated him beyond measure.

It was twisted and bent, like a shrub caged to grow in the shape of a horse. Not inherently bad, but wrong all the same. He made note of the scent of it. The taste and the feel. His mother would want an accurate description when he informed her.

Drawing his eyes from the lush red fabric of the tent, he was almost to the simple pink and white wagon when he felt the tingle of unease on his neck. Looking around, he couldn't quite pinpoint what had caused it, but he'd walked the earth long enough to trust his senses. Hoping to sink into the shadows and suss out his discomfort, he stepped around a small cart laden with trinkets of all shapes and sizes. Woolen foxes nestled alongside colored glass tiaras and copper cups sandwiched between pasteboard caricatures. The calliope music swelled, and Darkness's attention was drawn to a large carousel. He'd never seen its like before, and certainly old Elwell hadn't employed something so impressive.

Rather than a circle of parading horses, the mounts on the merry-go-round were an assortment of creatures born from both dreams and nightmares. The colors were vibrant, and each creature sported a tarnished silver saddle to match the pole driven through its core. There were horned goblins and raven-winged griffons. A pair of mers in matching crowns and a set of antlered rabbits. He counted three selkies in various transitions from seal to man and just as many larger-than-life nixies. Perhaps most intriguing of all, a massive teal and black kelpie, jaws wide and eyes feral, chased a delicate winged pixie, terror stark on her face.

Darkness cocked his head and followed the music toward the hideous contraption. It had a particular feeling, like a lullaby with the words all changed. Not comforting, but familiar all the same.

Perhaps a ride would suit him.

He was steps from the fencing separating the carousel from the walkway when a gaggle of school boys darted in front of him. He nearly tripped and let out a low curse. When he looked up, the ride had started its slow turn and Darkness was able to shake thought back into his head. His business was with the confectionary, not the carousel. That wasn't quite right, he corrected himself. His business was with the uncanny magic and his mind was with the confectionary. Either way, he didn't need to waste time on a children's ride, no matter how intriguing it felt.

Righting himself and following the scent of caramel and chocolate, he regained his original path, only to be stopped once again. This time by raised voices and slurred threats.

He blew out a long breath and looked to the heavens.

Tucked back off the main thoroughfare was a smaller and cleverly positioned tent. It was a gorgeous deep teal with silvery constellations dusting its surface. A house of charms if he had to guess.

A small group of men—a trio in fact—very drunk and very loud, huddled around the entrance.

Three nitwits. Three drunks. Threes and threes. If a third group crossed his path, Darkness knew the night would end poorly. Perhaps Violence and Evil would join him after all.

The men were jeering and laughing at something in front of them. Their bodies blocked Darkness's view of whatever or whoever it was.

"Come on now. We paid good money to get in here. We'll expect the full show." The man in the middle, a good head shorter than his friends but twice as surly, slurred his words as he looked down in the neighborhood of his knees.

The man beside him wore a bright green neckerchief and matching cap. Green Cap clapped Surly on the shoulder, lost his balance, and nearly ended up on his ass. His mates turned their attention from whoever they'd been taunting long enough to laugh at his expense.

Darkness could only wonder at the volume of whiskey the men had consumed.

"As I've told ya," a voice like water over gravel replied, "this tent's closed up for night."

Should have left well enough alone. They were distracted and laughing no longer.

"Aye. Aye. Fair enough then. Just give us back our coin and we'll call it all even." Spittle glistened on the surly lout's lips.

Darkness remained in the shadows, watching the exchange unfold. His eyes cast about, checking for his brother. This was just the sort of thing Violence would be drawn to.

"I'm afraid I don't carry the coin. Take your complaints to the ticket booth." The showman's voice showed no sign of fright. He'd likely dealt with this sort many times over.

"Bunch of dirty cheats. The lot of ya," Surly grumbled.

The man hidden in the shadows didn't possess Violence's keen sense of brutality, but it didn't take anything special to see where this was headed.

The last of the trio, a stocky man with a rather unfortunate face, raised one beefy fist as he stepped in front of his mates and took aim at the coinless showman. Darkness sighed and tilted his head back. Intervening in a brawl had not been on his list for the evening, but three against one was hardly sporting. He stepped out of the gloom as the man's clenched hand began its downward arc.

A step, a grab, and a grunt.

The succession was quick and ended with Darkness twisting his body and twirling the drunken fool's hand behind his back. He released the man and stepped back just as quickly, but the attacker was now several feet away from where he'd just stood. Rage dulled by significant inebriation flashed in the man's eyes as he realized he'd come nowhere close to landing a hit. He looked to Darkness, his eyes doing their best to focus. Darkness pursed his lips and cocked his head as he stared back at the man. The rage quickly turned to a confused sort of fear.

Darkness raised his brows and nodded, acknowledging the man's unease. "You heard the man, lads. Show's closed for the night."

The surly one in the middle bristled.

Darkness moved his gaze to him and crossed his arms.

It took no time at all for the man to look away. He turned and shambled off, his friends tight at his heels.

The showman, slight and willowy with a face that told stories of years on the road, sat cross-legged on a pillow at the tent's entrance. He removed a handkerchief from his breast pocket and wiped his face. He nodded his thanks to Darkness, but truth be told, he didn't look all too put out over either the threat of violence or the man who'd put a stop to it.

"It may be that we can keep the tent open a bit longer than expected. Reckon you'll be the last one in."

Darkness tsked. The showman might have done the same for the trio of drunks, had he been so inclined. Saved himself, and Darkness, a bit of unpleasantness.

"While I appreciate the offer, I've other plans this night."

"Ah, aye. Plenty to do. Plenty to do." Something behind Darkness caught the man's eye, and he grinned.

"All right then, Kerb?" The voice wasn't melodic. It was soft and worn with age. Nonetheless, it caught the dark man's attention. The way the consonants were rounded or the shape they took in the air perhaps. It was vaguely familiar yet completely unique.

Another peculiarity to add to the pile of them. His mind getting tricky. Knowing what he wanted and knowing just as well it couldn't be found.

He stiffened but didn't turn, keeping his back to the newcomer.

Kerb didn't move from his position on the pillow. He waved off the question. "O' course o' course, ladies. Right as rain. All's well that ends and all that."

"Ah, Kerb, you've got some company there." This voice was different. It had the same roundness to it, but the pitch was slightly higher, with more of a trill to it.

Darkness turned but pulled the shadows around himself, knowing he'd be visible but not identifiable in the gloom. He was met by a pair of aged ladies who could only be sisters. They had the same fair skin that had seen too many days of sun—freckled and lined. The same petite fragile frame, hunched at the shoulders. The same grey hair, though one wore it up in a knot at the top of her head and the other had hers cut in the style of a much younger woman. The same pale eyes, cloudy with time.

They stood arm in arm, studying him—or trying to at least.

He dipped his head. "Ladies."

"Ladies, he says. Well aren't you just the bees knees." The woman with the short hair smiled as she waved him off. "Why not step into the light, let us take your full measure then?"

"Afraid I'd be found lacking." He kept his voice low. It would do no good to frighten the pair. He still had work to do and had no mind to cause more of a stir than he already had.

"Oh, I doubt that very much." She angled her head and squinted, doing her best to get a look at him.

He stepped farther into the shadow. "Even so, I think I best be on my way."

"Suit yourself, but I'll have you know, there were times, and not so long ago mind you, that I'd have men like you lining up at my wagon each and every night. Isn't that right, Kerb?"

"Aye, and I was one of them." He beamed up at her. The woman chirped.

Darkness looked down at the man.

Kerb coughed. "Well, maybe not a man like you, but I was lined up anyhow. Still am."

"I imagine." Face still hidden, Darkness turned back to the women.

"I was just offering this gentleman a trip through the house of charms. He has declined my offer," Kerb said.

"Not many who'd do that." The woman with the short hair smiled. "Show's better in the big tent anyhow. A bit more enthralling but perhaps not quite as daring."

"I'll head that way then." Darkness made to leave, but something about the second woman made him pause. She hadn't spoken again, so he couldn't say it was her voice. As far as he knew, he'd never met her, but the familiarity niggled at him. She wore the puzzled look of someone who'd lost a thread of thought and knew it, frustrated they can't catch and weave it back into the correct order.

"Have you lost something, mistress?" He kept his voice low.

She shook her head. "No, I don't think. . . It's only that. . ."

"What's gotten into you?" her companion asked.

He had that effect on people, but this felt different. There was something about her voice.

"No, mistress? Are you certain? Perhaps a coin purse or the like?"

She only shook her head.

He wanted to hear her speak again, see if he could tease it out. "Your companion suggests the big top. And what about you, mistress? What attractions would you recommend?"

"Mistress? Such an odd thing to say. . ." She blinked, shaking her head as if to clear whatever thoughts she was having.

"Is it?" He twisted his lips.

"Isn't it?" She frowned. "Well, nevermind one way or the other. The cherry-lime bonbons."

Now it was his turn to frown. "What of them?"

"You asked what I'd recommend. The cherry-lime bonbons. At the confectionery. They're magical. Everyone should sample them at least once in their lifetime."

"Noted." He smoothed the frown from his face and inclined his head toward them. "It's been a joy."

Cherry-lime bonbons indeed. The night smacked of reminders. Still keeping to the shadows, Darkness turned and headed the way he'd come, the sweets wagon dead in his sights.

Only hours later did he acknowledge to himself how disappointed he'd been when the wagon of sugary treats had been closed up for the night. It was a shame. Cherry-lime bonbons were. . . It didn't matter. Instead, he visited the big top and strolled through the stalls of chance and the house of mirrors. The mirror maze brought its own set of memories flooding back, but not in the way the taste of citrus and sugar would have.

He never found what it was he sought. Just like the bonbons, the source of the magic alluded him. He was left with only the grim reminders of what had once been his.

He'd been sitting near the entrance when he thought he caught a ripple of magic, but it was gone before he could trace its source.

Finally, he gave up and vowed to leave the past buried where it belonged. He'd tell his mother of the magic and then he'd be done with it. She could send Violence and Evil to look further if she chose. No more carnival nights for him.

As he was leaving the grounds, a trio of men stumbled past.

Threes and threes. Never a good portent.

They were stooped and wrinkled—each of them just steps from the grave and certainly not the sort one generally saw at the carnival. They walked on shaky legs and supported each other in a feeble attempt to leave the carnival proper. That alone wasn't what bothered Darkness.

It took several long moments before he realized. As they ambled on, a breeze swooped in and clutched at the cap one of the men wore, sending it tumbling before them. A bright green cap to match the old man's bright green neckerchief.

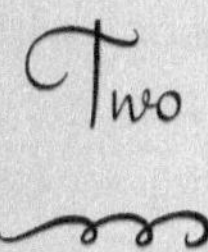

Two

Bronwen woke with a start, completely disoriented and overwhelmed by the oil and mothballs. The strength of the combination made her head thump, and she struggled to recall why she'd be smelling of it. She had no recollection of working any of the mechanical attractions or of being in the costume bins.

The more she tried to focus on the puzzle, the harder her head hurt. What was worse, not only was the previous night a blank, holes were scattered *everywhere* in her mind. She knew her name and knew where she was. She knew she was a candymaker and knew she loved birdsong. But fine details? No. Where her memories should have been was simply a swirling mass of light and color. Combined with the overpowering acrid stench, the effort brought a queasiness she didn't care for.

With a groan, she dislodged her cheek from a pillow damp with her own drool and rolled to take in her surroundings. Despite all the small peculiarities that felt just a touch off, she was certainly in her own wagon. She knew the fresh daisies were her favorite flower but didn't recognize the can in which they rested. She felt the curtains were her preferred shade of goldenrod but thought they should be linen rather than the heavy velvet that hung from the bar. A small collection of stones she couldn't recall collecting were positioned with care on the sill next to her bed along with a small purple sachet she didn't recall buying. And perhaps most startling, perched on the worn settee and studying her closely was a very pretty girl who looked only vaguely familiar.

"Finally," the girl said with a dramatic roll of her eyes. "I thought you'd never wake up."

Bronwen rubbed at her eyes. It did nothing to clear her mind. "Sorry. Who're you?"

Her voice sounded different in her own head. Crisper. Somehow stronger than it should.

The girl smiled and went from pretty to stunning in the blink of an eye. "Oh, come on, Winnie. You don't recognize your own sister?"

"Sister?" Did she have a sister? It seemed like something she should know, but even if she did, this girl was far too young to be her sister. Great-niece? Maybe. Sister? No.

She ran a hand down her face. "I'm in no mood and no mind for games."

She looked around. Her neck felt stiff, but that was nothing new.

Great age gaps aside, she wasn't too concerned that she couldn't recall. It was odd, the calm she felt in her confusion. She was old and sometimes old folks lost their marbles. It was a fact of life. She'd always been relatively sharp, but it seemed her age was finally catching up with her. The odd bit was that the young woman sitting there smiling brightly didn't seem the least bit concerned that she was addled.

The pretty young woman nodded. "Your one and only." She stood and stepped to the bed. "Up you get then." Her grip was firm as she pulled Bronwen to her feet. Even though her legs were loose and rubbery, she didn't fear a fall, such was the young woman's grip.

"That's my girl. You'll feel a peach in no time, I promise. We'll get some breakfast and take a stroll and things will start to clear."

The way she said it, simple and unwavering, had Bronwen feeling it must be true. Perhaps this was a dance the pair did often. She'd heard of those up in years who didn't remember a wink—their loved ones strangers to them. Perhaps she was one of those. She couldn't say, but she had a *feeling* they'd done this all before.

It took only the barest tug to get her in motion.

"Why do I reek of mothballs?"

"That'll be your clothes. Needed something with a better fit. A bit fresher, you know?"

"Fresher? Have you smelled this?" She pulled at her blouse.

"Let me help you with your boots." The girl—Bronwen refused to believe such a fresh-faced thing could be her sister —knelt down and guided her stockinged feet into a sturdy pair of leather boots. They were well worn and had dark smudges of stains across the toes. As she tied the laces, the girl chatted happily about the cook, his amazing hot buns, and how they were loading the train that very day for their next stop.

Was she meant to know where the next stop was? She hadn't the foggiest. Nor did she care at the moment.

"Sorry," she cut into the chattering. "But what's your name?"

"Oh, saints and sinners." The girl put a hand to her forehead and clasped both of Bronwen's hands in her own. "I'm a huge dolt, aren't I? Enid. I'm Enid. Do you remember that now, Winnie?" And strangely enough, as soon as the words left her lips—not only her own name, but also the familiar nickname she had for Bronwen—the memories came trickling back. Some of them at least.

Enid, her bubbly, beautiful, vivacious sister. As a young woman, fearless and graceful as she flew above the crowds in the big top. How could she have forgotten? Crowds came just to see her up on the trapeze. Strong and firm and glorious. In her prime, no one could compete.

But that was all in the past. Enid hadn't soared over a crowd in years.

In. Years.

And here she stood before her. Young.

Enid. Young.

Enid standing before her. Young.

Bronwen glanced at their joined hands.

It couldn't be. Her own hands were just as youthful and smooth as Enid's.

She stumbled to the small mirror on her desk. Blinking rapidly, she raised a shaking hand to her cheek.

Blink. A perfectly smooth hand on a perfectly rosy cheek.

Blink, blink. Clear shining eyes.

Blink. Blink, blink. Gnarled knuckles and age spots gone.

Blink. Hair smooth and silky, not a wiry strand to be seen.

Blink. Blink. Blink. Shoulders straight and wrinkles gone.

Bronwen as she'd been decades before. Staring back at her in the small reflective glass. Looking just as young and vibrant and fresh as Enid.

Although her little sister was ten months younger, many took them for twins. They shared the same thick dark blonde hair and apple cheeks. The same full lips and large grey eyes. She knew all of this, but seeing the Enid of the past right next to her same youthful face was the most unsettling thing to have happened since she woke.

"Am I dreaming?"

Enid shook her head.

"Are you certain?"

"I could pinch you if you like." There was a twinkle in her eye.

"It's just . . . how?"

"You know how, Winnie. You just need to let it come to you. It always does. The confusion will subside."

It *always* does?

This had happened before.

In her gut, she knew that it had. The knowledge filled her with dread.

It wasn't right. *This* wasn't right.

Either Enid didn't pick up on her distress or she simply chose to ignore it. "Come on. Let's get some breakfast. The gang's all anxious to see you."

Bronwen stopped herself from being pulled out the door. "I don't understand."

"I know." Enid blew out an exasperated breath. At least her impatience hadn't changed. "Just trust me, all right."

She gave a not-so-gentle tug and pulled Bronwen down the wooden steps of the wagon and onto the still dew-damped grass. Sounds of waking surrounded them. Doors creaking, animals braying, and somewhere in the distance a mallet striking wood.

She looked around and was immediately grateful for the sight of the bright pink and white wagon parked next to the slightly larger wagon she'd just exited. Swirling loops of filagree surrounded the word CONFECTIONARY on the side. Inside would be her kettle and stove, sacks of sugar and nuts, flour and bars of cocoa. It was where she worked her own brand of magic, creating delicate treats and childhood memories.

The two wagons didn't normally sit together. This she knew. Like all of the troupe's accommodations, her wagon— the one she'd lived in, slept in, read in, and traveled in for her entire life—was never out among the attractions. Correction —not *her* wagon. *Their* wagon. The one she shared with Enid. Their wagon was never amid the attractions. Her confections wagon, however, always was.

Enid had mentioned they were moving out, and it looked as though her pink and white wagon was on its way to being loaded.

A pair of broad stocky men were grasping the crossbar. With practiced efficiency they continued leading it away and toward one of many flat train cars waiting on the tracks nearby. Soon it, along with all the other wagons and tents and stalls, would be loaded and ready for the train to pull out on its way to the next stop.

The aroma of coffee and bacon grease filled the air as they approached a ring of worn wooden chairs, several of which were occupied by men and women of various shapes, sizes, and ages.

"Morning, ladies."

"Hiya, Kerb," Enid responded to a thin older man who was busy shoveling potatoes and eggs onto a dented tin plate.

The food was simple fare as was the long pine board it rested upon. Wooden sawhorses held the makeshift table in place.

"Don't be shy now. Fill up a plate. I'll wager your appetite is a might bit bigger than it's been in a time." He winked at Bronwen and grabbed a tin cup and headed to an empty chair.

He was right. She was suddenly ravenous. She did as directed and took a worn-looking dish and piled it high with food—warm brown bread, eggs, and tomatoes. Even a scoop of baked beans in a savory sauce. She looked around and found two empty seats then tucked into the meal.

She'd eaten half of her plate before Enid strolled over and handed her a much-needed mug of strong hot tea. "Just the way you like it."

Bronwen took a tentative sip, closed her eyes, and sighed deeply. The girl was right. The bitter brew was tempered with cream and a good dose of sugar. The fact that she'd nearly blistered her tongue didn't matter. It was heavenly.

Not eager to ruin the moment, the pair sat in silence while Bronwen blew over the rim until she could comfortably down most of the mug.

"Feel better?" Enid's eyes twinkled.

"I'm not worse."

"I suppose that'll do for now."

Bronwen looked around the smattering of chairs and their occupants. She recognized some of the faces watching her expectantly. Others were complete strangers, but she got the odd feeling if she studied them long enough, they too would come into focus. Odder still were the ones that were a peculiar amalgamation of old familiar faces transposed on young fresh ones. The overall effect made her head swim and her stomach knot.

"Close your eyes and just breathe deep, Winnie." Enid rested a hand on her shoulder and gave a gentle squeeze.

Bronwen did as she was told. She'd been doing quite a bit of that this morning, and she wasn't certain she liked it.

Still, she closed her eyes and sat quietly, breathing in the fresh morning air for more than a minute. The gentle burble of voices mixed with the bird chatter and clattering of dishes was familiar and soothing. By the time she opened her eyes, she felt not quite herself but a good deal closer to it.

Curious eyes and knowing smiles still darted her way, but rather than feeling uncomfortable or menacing, she recognized them for the friendly hopeful things they were. She might be confused, but she knew in her heart, these were her people.

"Finish up and we'll take a stroll." Enid nodded to Bronwen's plate even as she shoveled a forkful of eggs into her mouth. "That'll help." The words were a mumbled mess around her breakfast. She took a gulping slug of tea. "CJ'll want to be seeing you this morning before we head on."

Enid was raising the mug to her lips when she stopped midway and laughed. "Saints and sinners, Winnie. It's only CJ."

Bronwen realized she was frowning, but she couldn't say why. The name was familiar, just as Enid's had been. The identity of its owner however was dancing just out of her reach.

"It'll be quick. We're set to head out at midday. I'm excited, but to be honest, I was hoping to get in some training today. Loosen up these muscles, you know?"

Bronwen did not in fact know. In her estimation it had been nearly twenty years since Enid had even thought about training or loosening up anything.

"Where to?" She'd rather think about the next stop than try to tease out why this CJ person made her feel so nervous or what exactly Enid was talking about or any of a dozen other things.

Even if she didn't know what precisely was happening, Bronwen still knew the circuit. The tiny villages and more bustling towns that dotted the countryside. She knew how long it would take to travel from the city in the south— where they hit once a year for repairs as well as sequins, feathers, and any number of paints and materials—to each of their regular appointments. She knew which towns to avoid and where they might do quite well. She knew the number of hours the whole show could be hoisted and how quickly it could be torn down and packed up. She knew what her sweets would sell for and when to hide her coins. Even sitting there, she could perfectly recall the recipe for honey cakes and how to get the perfect texture of caramel to coat her apples. None of that had been lost behind the fog in her mind.

The circuit was in her bones.

It was equal parts comforting and terrifying—knowing what she had and what so clearly had been lost.

Enid tucked her lower lip between her teeth and raised her eyebrows. "Feyport." As soon as she spoke the word, her face broke into a devilish grin. Bronwen couldn't contain her own answering smile.

Another odd thing to remember. The tiny seaside village had only adopted the moniker recently, but she knew exactly where they were headed. A lovely little spot with a lovely bunch of folks. Folks who, as the name suggested, welcomed all sorts of visitors.

"I know, right. Can't think of a better place to show off the refurbishments." Enid waggled her eyebrows.

Bronwen's frown deepened. *The refurbishments.* Enid obviously meant it as a joke, but the statement had the opposite effect. It sent a queasy feeling rolling through Bronwen. Again, Enid clearly didn't notice.

"I was chatting with some of the girls yesterday. It's going around that there are not only selkies frequenting Feyport, but some fairies and even a warlock or two. They've had pookas and nixies and a girl with honest-to-bonkers antlers." She drained the last from her mug and stood. "I've always wanted to meet a selkie, Winnie. Maybe this is my chance."

Bronwen nodded but continued to frown. When had Enid ever wanted to meet a selkie? The longer she'd spent with Enid that morning, the more she was remembering about her sister. The memories weren't exactly flooding her; they just seemed to gradually reappear when she wasn't paying attention. The fog wasn't exactly thinning, but it was breaking up into great patches of lost memories interspersed with perfects bits of clarity. She knew Enid was in love with the idea of being in love. Always had been. She would flit from one young man to the next easier than changing her shoes. And while she often had her cards read and left gifts out for the sprites, she'd never really been into magic. This was more likely her being dramatic just for the sake of it.

But she couldn't be sure, and it would surely drive her mad.

Was the woman with gnarled knuckles and failing vision all some false memory? A trick of the mind? Perhaps this was all some odd fever dream and she would awake at any moment, achy and gray once more.

But Enid had never lacked confidence. That she was sure of. Her sister said the memories would return, and so far she'd been right. Bronwen just needed to to trust her, even if she couldn't recall this desire to meet a magical seal man. In the meantime, she supposed it was time to get on with things.

It was time to go see CJ.

Her tinplate clattered as she dropped it into the bin with the others and followed her sister through the loose gathering of showmen and women.

The morning was cool and pleasant, the grass moist with dew and smelling just as it ought—all green and earthy. Hints of animal dung mingled with traces of popped corn, rich roasted peanuts, and sticky sweet sugar. It smelled like home.

Her heart had settled a bit, either because of the return of some of her memories or despite them, but as they neared the sleek black train carriage, her pulse began to spike. Just minutes earlier, she couldn't place who CJ was, but with every step closer, the picture of him grew firmer in her mind. She recalled him as a young man, tall and spindly with a mind made for the circuit and a drive to match. And then older, wiser but still just as driven. He was aged and soft in her mind now, but then again so was she.

He was more a brother than an employer, and that thought left her feeling not only confused but guilty. How could she be afraid of CJ? It made no sense.

She'd known him for years. They'd traveled the circuit

countless times and dozens of years together. He'd always taken care of the troupe—paid fair wages, kept security tight, and didn't overwork any of them. He'd given her sound advice anytime she'd asked for it but didn't overstep when she kept to herself.

So why was she dreading seeing him?

And then it hit her. If she walked onto that train car and the man she expected to see wasn't old and worn, it would be bad. It would mean her mind was cracking. If he *was* the old man she expected, she might get some answers.

"You're fretting, Winnie. I've told you, there's no need to fret."

Enid mounted the small ladder to the back of the car and stepped to the side to allow Bronwen room to follow. With a loud click, the door opened and the sisters stepped inside.

Pipe smoke filled the familiar space. Red velvet benches and polished wood cabinets lined the back half before ending in a wall housing shelves and drawers fitted with shining chrome knobs. A polished door opened on one side of the wall, and a thin impeccably dressed man stepped through.

Bronwen breathed in. Whether in relief or dismay, she couldn't decide. CJ Colger smiled at her, and despite the youthful twinkle in his eyes, he was just as she remembered— thinning white hair, pipe-stained teeth and all.

"Bronwen, my dear. Look. At. You!" He clapped with each word.

"Hello, CJ."

He stepped forward, stork-like legs strong and steady despite their appearance. Bronwen let herself be enfolded in his embrace, the wiry hairs of his expertly trimmed beard tickling her cheek. She could feel his ribs under his waistcoat and wondered how he could still have the energy to continue running the show.

Pushing her back a step but keeping his knobly hands on her arms, he studied her.

"How are you feeling?"

"Fine I suppose. But. . ."

"But a touch bewildered?" He released her arms and tapped a finger to his temple.

"Sure. Bewildered. As good a word as any, I suppose."

"As I am confident Enid has told you, it will all come back eventually."

"Yes, she's said that." Bronwen looked over her shoulder to where Enid reclined on one of the velvet benches, twirling a short lock of honey blonde hair around her finger.

"And when you do, you'll not only understand, you'll thank me."

"Thank you?" She frowned. Feeling uneasiness once again growing in her stomach, she shook her head. "This isn't me, CJ. I was . . . we were." She needed to just get it out there. "We were old, CJ. I know that sounds like I've taken a knock to the head, but I remember it."

"Of course you do." As he grinned, Bronwen couldn't help the shiver that ran from the base of her skull all the way to her toes. "Because, Bronwen dear, you were."

"How?" The word came out sharp. Accusing. And then softer, near tears, "Why?"

CJ's lips tightened. "As I've said, it will all come back." The words were clipped and tight. Any warmth he'd held in his eyes was gone.

"You can't just tell me?"

"I've found it can be quite jarring. Best if you come to it on your own. In the meantime, you must simply enjoy your newfound youth."

At that moment, Bronwen wasn't certain she could enjoy anything.

"Now, as I am sure you can imagine, we've got to get a

move on. And as you've probably seen, we're stretched a bit thin this week. We had to let a good number of the troupe go as of late. If we are to keep our timetable, the train must depart in"—he pulled a gleaming silver pocket watch from his waistcoat—"just under two hours." He snapped it shut and replaced it in his pocket. "I have such high hopes for our next stop. I'm meeting a man about a new addition to the show, and if I am not mistaken, that won't be the only bright point. I have a feeling the folks there will be a wonderful pick-me-up for us all."

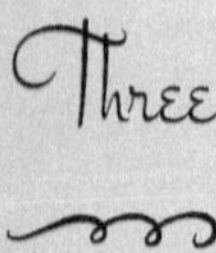

Three

The Witch Carman wasn't easily troubled.

She was, however, easily vexed.

"If it keeps coming down like this, I'll be replanting half the garden."

Darkness shook rain from his hair and grimaced at the woman standing just inside the doorway. His mother was feared far and wide, and not without cause. In that moment however, standing, staring out into the yard, bronze hair and olive skin gleaming, she looked more a simple young farm lass than a centuries-old witch. Her appearance suggested they might be siblings—not mother and son.

She held the door for him more out of habit than concern. It was the garlic scapes and the blueberries and the yew she was fretting over. Not her dripping and shivering son.

"The herbs are just so fragile."

"Yes. So I'm told." He dropped into a chair by the fire and stretched out his long legs. With any luck, his boots at least would dry by the time he was sent out again. For all that he could control the very light needed to see by, he was no match for a good downpour.

She didn't look at him, absorbed as she was by the rain and the wind and the thyme. "Oh, my boy. You're in a mood."

He grunted but didn't argue. One did well not to argue with *The Witch*.

"You know, I expect this type of thing from your brother, not from you."

"This type of thing being?"

With a last frown out the door, she shut it and wiped her hands on the simple apron she wore. "You know what I speak of."

"All right then. Which brother?"

"Which brother?" She flicked her hand at him as if to flick away his foolishness. "Dain of course." Dain. Violence. That narrowed it down at least. "Dother would never deign to ignore what you so willingly do."

Darkness tilted his head back on the chair and closed his eyes. "And what evil is it I am turning a blind eye to?"

"Not evil, per se. That's being a bit dramatic. Let's call it something wicked."

He knew she was watching him. Testing him. Waiting for him to jump to whatever game she wanted to play. He remained in his chair, heedless to the water soaking into the cushions. His eyes placidly closed.

"Yes, that's it. Wicked."

He couldn't help it. He grunted.

"Come now, Dub, I know you can sense it. This storm isn't natural. Not the right season for it." To emphasize her point, lightning flashed and was quickly followed by a booming crack of thunder. "See. Not natural."

"Yes, Mother. You of all would know."

"If I didn't know better, I'd think you had something on your mind. Something you'd like to discuss?"

"Not at present." He was concerned but would never admit it to her.

The carnival had stopped in Feyport after all. He'd told her about the odd magic he'd sensed, but deep down he really had hoped it would stay away from the quaint village she so adored.

"Really? Hmm. It's just that you seem . . . well, let's just say I hope you aren't entertaining any of that foolishness again."

"What foolishness would that be?" He sat up straighter and looked at her.

"Oh, you know." She fluttered her hand in the air. "That whole thing you went through some years back."

"I have no idea of what you are referring." He *did* know of course. It was always there. That longing. And even if he could shove it aside, his family would never let him forget it.

"Hmm. Well, no matter. There is work to be done."

He sighed and rubbed again at his brow.

"Why must you plague me so?" Carman asked.

"I've told you. I am not going. Send Dother."

"He'll only make it worse. You of all would know."

He groaned as she played his own words back on him.

"It would be much easier if you'd do this willingly." Of course it would be. In the end, she'd get what she wanted. She always did. "I'll send for Dain. He can accompany you."

Darkness rubbed his hands over his eyes and opened them to find his mother smiling at him in victory.

Four

❧

Crafting lollipops wasn't Bronwen's favorite thing. For one, it was quite a bit harder than many folks realized. The sugar needed to be precisely the perfect temperature and mixed with precisely the right amount of water; otherwise, the candy wouldn't set quite right. No one wanted a lolly that was too brittle or too gooey or too cloudy. Then there was the physicality of it. She didn't mind a bit of hard work, but this candy was sticky and hot and there was so much waiting only to be followed by a mad dash at just the right moment. After endless minutes watching the boiling pot, the molds needed to be filled quickly and the sticks placed just so.

And *always* the need to avoid getting boiling glop on her hands. She'd had her share of burns in the past.

Lollipops sold by the bucket though, so make them she would. Right after she finished her second least favorite confection: delicately patterned hard sweets designed to look like stained glass. Those needed to be pulled and stretched, rolled and thinned. Cut into nuggets that showed the beautiful pattern only to be sold for less than pennies a handful.

It was a brutal dance but one Brownen did willingly.

The rain certainly didn't help. They'd done well to place the large waxed canvas flaps up around her outdoor kitchen. It kept the bulk of the rainwater from dumping into the kettles and from running into her molds. The fires were able to stay lit, but the air was still thick and heavy. It was messing with the temperatures and making her recipes slightly off. She'd needed to pay extra attention to each small detail to keep heaps of sugar from being ruined by the deluge.

Rain or shine, however, the show must go on.

She'd finished two large batches of mouthwatering and decadent fudge, filled to bursting with nuts and worth every bit of toil in the making. The fudge had been after the marshmallows, and the marshmallow had been after the candied fruit, and the candied fruit had been after the sweet little sugar mice that were nearly too adorable to actually eat. Once she had the hard candies and lollies cooling, she could move on to her favorites, the cakes and puddings. If the rain let up, the caramel-coated popping corn and the candy floss would be last minute before the ticket booths began admitting the patrons. She'd do several batches of those repeatedly throughout the night. The smell of all that cooking sugar would do more for her business than anything else. If it continued to be more than a drizzle however, the floss would be out. It would melt as soon as the water hit it.

The copper drum kettle wasn't enormous by any stretch. There simply wasn't enough room in the wagon for anything the size of the ones she'd admired when visiting the city, but Bronwen's was still a hefty thing. Particularly when it was filled with bubbling molten sugar.

"Ready, Tommy?" she asked the young man at her side.

His sandy curls dripped water onto his face.

Another recently recovered memory—Tommy was her favorite hand when she needed assistance.

He'd been one of the first carnival folks she'd remembered clearly, aside from Enid and CJ.

She'd been so happy to have his help. They were short on hands still, CJ insisting they would take more on after the next stop and would just need to make do until then. She knew several other attractions could use his skills, but she wasn't going to give him up easily.

He was a big strapping lad about her same age—or at least the age she currently appeared—with a crooked smile and arms the size of small tree trunks. He had a vicious scar that ran the length of his forehead and kind earnest eyes. Thankfully, she had no memory of him as any age other than how he currently appeared. What that meant, she wasn't sure. She just knew it was a comfort to have him helping her and not thinking of him as anything other than helpful.

He never spoke but was quick to assist and followed instructions to the most minute detail.

With a grunt from her and a grin from him, the pair lifted the copper tub and poured the contents into the waiting molds. A waft of sugary steam filled the air as Bronwen retrieved a handful of woven paper sticks from her pocket and placed them quickly yet squarely in the hot candy.

Despite the humidity, the flattened discs would harden and make a handheld treat sure to satisfy any sweet tooth.

Another task done but still so much to do. It was a *good* busy. A *good* pressure.

Being task oriented took concentration. That concentration was funneled directly into the tasty morsels so many fair-goers would seek out. And while her mind was immersed in pulling sugar and boiling fudge, it couldn't be centered on the wrongness of her age and the fact that she was both mortified and pleased that she had the energy to double her production from just weeks prior.

Tommy popped back and forth from her open air kitchen

to various other tasks the troupe demanded of him. Like so many of them, he wasn't a performer. He provided muscle for opening and tearing down and served as a kind of security presence should things get out of hand as they were occasionally want to do.

Each time he returned to her, he washed his hands in the barrel beside her wagon even though the rain had him soaking from tip to toe. At least he didn't seem to mind, giving her a grin each time he was ready for a new duty.

"What else have they got you on today, Tommy?" She was busy cutting sponge cake and had to look up to see him gesture. He ran his hand in a flat swirling motion, his face grim.

"The carousel?" she asked.

He nodded, looking even more uncomfortable.

"Don't worry. I don't like it either," Bronwen said flatly.

A blank expression crossed his face, and he frowned.

"What? You don't believe me?"

He shrugged, the frown easing just a bit.

She wasn't sure why, but the need to explain to him was strong. "Tommy. I do not like the carousel. As far as I can remember, I have never liked it. It's . . . I don't know. A bit sinister, I suppose."

Frankly, she was surprised more of the troupe didn't feel the same way. It was eerie. All those creatures with their lurid grins or terrified, pained expressions. Patrons loved it. It gave them that sense of danger they came looking for, but it felt off to her.

He nodded but still looked unconvinced. She didn't understand why he should doubt her.

"You don't like the beastly thing, Tommy, so why on earth should you think I would?"

He gave a half shrug and tilted his head then ran a finger in a circle around his face and pointed to hers.

"My face?"

He nodded.

"Saints and sinners. What's my face got to do with anything?"

Tommy chewed on the inside of his lip and cast a glance around in search of a way to explain.

There was no immediate help for him.

"Shall I fetch the chalk?"

Bronwen kept a small slate and bits of chalk handy so Tommy could write questions he had about the jobs she gave him. They didn't often need it anymore, adept as he'd become in anticipating her needs. They still had much to do, but with his help, she was certain they'd be properly stocked come gate drop, and more importantly, she was quite intrigued by what he could tell her.

He nodded, obviously just as keen to share his thoughts as she was to receive them.

She pointed to the canvas above them. "Make sure the rain stays off this sponge then."

She was two steps toward her wagon when a high-pitched wail broke over them. It was followed by a series of indecipherable shouts, and then all over the grounds, mayhem broke loose.

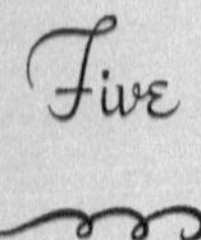

Five

"I don't like it," Darkness said as he walked toward the field of bustling showmen and women.

"Aye. I'm aware," Violence answered.

"Why not just come back tonight when it opens properly?"

"Where's the fun in that, brother?"

"I didn't realize we were meant to be having fun, *brother*."

"Oh aye. O' course we are. It may not be the entire goal, but why not relish in it when we can? And no use pretending you aren't having a delicious time. We all know how you enjoy the carnival."

Darkness stopped and turned to Violence. The storm hadn't yet let up, and rain dripped from the leaves all around them. It was no match for the storm he felt inside at his brother's words.

It must have shown. Violence held his hands up in mock surrender. The rain plastered his white hair to his skull and the clouds darkened his glacial eyes to grey. "Careful now, brother. I sense you may do something rash, and as much as I'll enjoy it, now isn't the time." He smirked, and Darkness had to resist the urge to wrap his hands around the offending man's throat.

Violence was, after all, correct. He would enjoy the interaction far too much, even if he was on the receiving end of the attack. Just as Dub was drawn to and could manipulate the gloom and the dark, Dain was a master of the brutality of others. He could feed on the savagery or just revel in his ability to amplify it depending on his mood.

Darkness wouldn't give him the satisfaction.

Hands fisted at his sides, he walked farther into the trees. "Let's just see what can be seen and then be done with this business."

"See what can be seen. Smell what can be smelled. Hear what can be heard. Yes, yes," Violence agreed.

"And then be done," Darkness emphasized.

"Perhaps."

Darkness didn't need to look at his brother to know a grin was in his eyes and on his lips.

"But what of tasting? Surely there will be some sweet treat you'd like to try."

Darkness fisted his hand even tighter.

Violence's laugh was nothing short of gleeful.

Darkness hadn't always been so on edge. He'd worked hard to feel as little as possible in fact. But recently the feel of the night had changed, and then there'd been the smell on the wind. The sugar and shadows entwining as if they could never be parted.

He didn't like the idea of that. Not a bit. Not the memories it evoked. Not the feelings it tortured him with. Not what it had meant ages ago nor what it would never mean again.

"Dub. Brother. Ease your mind. It's only meant in jest." Violence clapped him on the shoulder, sending droplets of water in every direction.

Darkness grunted.

They walked on in silence for another handful of minutes. Loud clanging and the sounds of men laboring began to overtake the sounds of rain pattering on the leaves. Metal on wood and the higher pitch of metal on metal rang out. Animal sounds too. Horses and more exotic things—things that had no business in this part of the world—sent their calls up.

Ahead, the trees broke just enough to create the illusion of a long green tunnel.

They were near the old sheep farm that was set to house the carnival for their stay. Old manure, briny salt air, hay and the sweat of toiling men mixed with the rain to create an earthy miasma.

"Well, this isn't exciting at all." Violence had stopped at the edge of the trees and stood arms crossed surveying the scene. "It's not at all as I remember it."

"Centuries tend to change things."

"I suppose they do. You yourself are nothing as you were."

Darkness didn't need to be reminded.

The brothers stood side by side, postures and expressions nearly identical. More out of habit than anything else, Darkness pulled the gloom in around them both, shielding them from any who might wonder at the pair.

He needn't have worried. The men and woman of the carnival were focused on their tasks, putting up tents and erecting great metal structures designed to awe and entertain. Big burly men and thin willowy teens tugged and pulled and hammered their amusements into form. Trouser-clad women and young pock-faced boys darted in and out while others fed livestock and a stout middle-aged man crooned soothing words to a pair of pacing jungle cats.

The cats were not soothed. They were, however, the only creatures to sense the brothers lurking on the edge of the woods. One let up a yowl only to be matched immediately by its fellow.

"Now those I approve of. We should let them out, don't you suppose," Violence said.

"Not everything must be brawls and murderous affairs," Darkness replied.

"No, but a little murder does liven things up."

They watched as the carnival grew from haphazard piles of canvas, wood, and steel to a wonderland of small booths and alleyways, tents and attractions.

At length, Violence asked, "So where do you suppose this magical source resides, then?"

"I can't say. I thought for certain it would be under the big top, but I got no sense of anything overly strong when I visited it."

"Took in a show, did you?"

Darkness didn't bother with a reply.

"You're ever so tense these days." Violence sighed. "And nothing else seemed extraordinary?"

The confectionery. The same pink and white stripes. The same gilded lettering.

But he'd not say that to his brother and bring about more less-than-subtle jabs.

"I told Mother. I couldn't find it."

"Yes. Yes, I know. But there must have been something that felt different."

The tickle of the familiar yet twisted magic. Where was he when he'd felt it?

"The carousel," Darkness said at last.

"Come again?" Violence raised a single white eyebrow.

"There was this carousel. My mind was being . . . tricky. But now I recall the carousel."

"A children's ride? Oh, Dub." He sighed. "Well, what of it?"

"That carousel was made for no child I know. Well, save Dother perhaps when he was small."

Just as with the shadows for Dub and life's brutality for Dain, Dother was keenly in tune with evil in all its earthly forms. Unlike his brothers however, his affinity wasn't something he took comfort in. It was more a duty that often left him needing chunks of time away from others, including his family.

Violence flicked his eyes to Darkness. "Interesting."

"It was in a way."

"Explain."

"It had a weight to it. A draw. And this was no normal carousel filled with prancing ponies or colorful timidity. It had teeth."

"Well then," Violence said with a grin. "Let us go in search of the thing."

"Ah. And here we find something worth seeing." Violence didn't bother to lower his voice or duck out of sight. No man, or woman for that matter, was enough to make him hide when he was in a mood to be seen. Darkness knew his brother was on occasion fond of sharing his shadows, but that was more for his own amusement than anything else.

Violence stood near a stack of half empty crates, the contents of which were being systematically unpacked by a team of showmen. The crew, focused on their task, didn't question the tall imposing man with the shock of white hair and glacial eyes.

Rain continued to fall, but it was easing up a bit. More a misting in the air than a steady drizzle.

Darkness let the shadows dissolve and stood next to his brother, dark head to his light, wondering how long it would take before they were noticed.

A pair of brawny men, shirts and faces wet from either sweat or rain, were affixing a saddled mer to the carousel. A long silver pole ran through her torso just between her shoulder blades and down to the carousel base. Her face was wide eyed and her arms thrust back, in a perpetual state of fleeing whatever mount would be placed behind her.

"You feel it, don't you?" Darkness asked.

"Aye, brother. I do."

"What do you make of it?" Darkness stared at the carousel. It was somehow more monstrous for the fact it was only partially built—magical creatures formed of plaster and metal lying dismembered on the ground, awaiting a shaft to run them through and place them in their never-ending chase.

"Surely you don't mean you don't know?"

At the confusion in his brother's voice, Darkness tore his gaze from the ride and looked at Violence. "I know it's strong and I know it's warped. What more am I meant to know?"

"You really don't, do you?" Violence laughed openly, the noise finally drawing attention from a couple of the showmen. "Oh, Dub." He wiped at his eyes.

"Hey! You there. You aren't meant to be here until the ropes drop later tonight."

The laughter died on Violence's lips as he focused on the man who'd spoken. "I think you'll find we can be just about anywhere we like." He nodded to the carousel. "Especially given what you toy with there."

The man took a step toward Darkness and Violence. "Look now, friend, I don't want to have to toss you out on your arse. Just take yourselves off and come back tonight like all the rest."

The showman wasn't a particularly large man, nor did he appear to be the angry sort spoiling for a fight. It was likely he was used to townsfolk trying to sneak in early. Kids most of the time if Darkness were to guess. The man clearly wasn't prepared for what he'd get with Violence.

"Don't tease me." Violence smiled and took a step forward.

The showman took a step back, his foot landing in a muddy puddle. He didn't seem to notice. "Don't want no trouble now. You fellas just need to let us do our job, and then you can come back and enjoy the show."

"And if we don't wish to just 'let you do your job'?" Violence took another step forward.

Darkness put a hand on his brother's shoulder. It was no time to play games. His brother didn't need to stir up trouble just for the fun of it all.

"Perhaps we should listen to the man, brother. Come back tonight as he suggests."

Violence shook him off. "I don't think so. So tell me, what if we'd rather stay? See what there is to see, so to speak."

The showman looked over his shoulder at his colleagues. "Well then, friend, I suppose we'll need to take matters into our own hands, won't we."

Violence smiled and caught his lower lip between his teeth as he shook his head.

The showman called out to his friends, drawing several more of them closer to the brothers.

Darkness silently cursed his brother but didn't move to leave.

"You bring that grotesqueness here, to the lands The Witch calls home, and you use promises of a fight. You better be willing to follow through. *Friend.*"

And then Darkness understood. The charm on the carousel was indeed twisted and wrong. But it was also famil-iar. He'd sensed it before, and being this close, now he knew it to be true. It was familiar because he'd once held it in his hands. Right after his mother had crafted the charm.

It was no longer the same bit of benign spellwork though. His mother would never have brought something so sinister into such a place.

He had no idea how it had become so warped. He had no idea how Colger & Sons had come into possession of it. He had no idea how it was bound to the carousel and for what purpose. He did know it was nothing good.

"It can't be the same charm." He didn't know who he was speaking to, but it was Violence who answered.

"Oh, brother. But it is. And she'll not be happy." He looked back to the small group of showmen. "Now. Let me have a little fun."

Darkness was certain Violence would have his fun and more, but as he moved to take on the ragtag group, a loud splashing sound was followed by an anguished cry and sounds of a man screaming.

The showmen turned in unison to a night-dark wagon adorned with frothy white waves.

A short stocky man cringed at the noise. "I knew the damn thing was a bad idea. She'll kill us all given the chance."

A loud wailing answered him, and the man threw his hands over his ears.

Violence and Darkness turned as one and stared at the wagon.

"What have we here? More and more and more to see. And now we are hearing what is to be heard, are we not?"

Darkness pulled his brother away from the fight he so evidently craved.

The uproar near the sea-coated wagon was growing. Loud splashes and men shouting could be heard from within. A loud wail that turned into a growl followed, and then things really got out of hand. The wagon rocked back and forth, and Darkness wondered if the wooden wheels would snap clean off.

"And what fresh act of terror goes on in there? I'm sure our new *friends* could tell us," Violence said.

But the men were already on the move. All save the one with his hands over his ears.

Violence took a step in his direction.

"Leave him," Darkness said over his shoulder as he followed the showmen closer to the wagon and the bedlam surrounding it.

The door at the rear of the thing swung open, and an elderly man with a crisp white beard and long spindly legs toppled out and down the steps. He caught himself just before his knees hit the rain-soaked grass and swore to no one in particular. Standing on shaking legs, he turned back to the wagon and shouted, "Not another man steps foot in that wagon. Do you understand me?"

Several of the showmen backed up, concern and confusion on their faces.

"Lucy. Enid. Get over here if you please." He pulled the cuffs of his shirt, straightening the sleeves as he looked at two young women who'd arrived at the spectacle.

"We have a very special guest inside that wagon. One I'd hoped to introduce to the troupe this evening, but as you can see, things aren't going quite as I'd planned and it looks as if you might be just the solution to my woes."

Pulling gloom around himself, Darkness skirted around the back of the wagon, hoping to get a better vantage through the door and into the wagon itself. Violence, rather than follow him, stalked right past the women and headed toward the wagon door.

"Enid? If you don't mind fetching your sister and perhaps one or two other hearty young women." And then he noticed Violence headed his way.

The old man gaped at the imposing figure bearing down on him.

Darkness cursed under his breath, knowing where this was going.

The distraction was too good an opportunity to pass up however. He pursed his lips and sent a look to his brother, silently begging him not to inflict too much damage, then stepped inside the wagon.

Rather than being a shelter from the rain, it felt as if he'd been submerged underwater. Damp and dank hung in the air. The space had been painted to look akin to a river bed— smooth stones in shades of taupe and brown on the lower walls, and water plants and beams of muted sunlight higher up the wagon walls. Hanging lanterns swayed with the settling movement of the wagon, causing light to dance on the wall and add to the feeling of being submerged in swiftly flowing water.

In the center, a large tank held residence. The corners were reinforced brass hinges holding thick glass walls in place. It stood a head taller than Darkness himself, leaving several feet between the tops of the walls and the ceiling of the wagon. A narrow set of wooden steps gave access to the tank on one side.

Darkness cursed.

It wasn't the tank itself that had anger rising in his veins. Nor was it the two lifeless bodies floating near the bottom— both showmen from the looks of their clothing—one young and trim, the other middle aged with a long beard that obscured his face as it drifted in the water. It was the woman surfacing to the top. Her hands were bound with a thick coil of rope, and a similar length attached her left foot to a hook in the bottom of the tank.

She broke the surface and flipped her long black tresses from her delicately featured face, revealing an angry grimace. "Oh, and what a handsome one they send me now."

Mavka. Naiad. River siren. *Rusalka*. Many names for the same trapped maiden.

"Oh, mistress. What have they done?" Darkness was aghast. This wonderous creature did not belong here. Not in a tank. And certainly not bound as she was.

"What have they done? What have you done? What matters who or what? All that matters now is what I will do."

He shook his head. "Your quarrel is not with me, mistress."

"You are a man, are you not? My quarrel is with all men."

Whoever had brought this woman there and thought a few lengths of hemp would be enough to subdue her was more than a fool.

"Not this man. And even if it were, I am sad to say, your gift will not work on me."

The hunger in her eyes was undeniable. "Are you so sure? Come closer and let us see."

"If I come closer, it will be to free you from this place. Nothing more and nothing less."

"Free me then and take me to the water. It's close. I can smell it." She tilted her head back, staring up at the ceiling as if it didn't exist and only the stars lay between her and a river of flowing fresh water.

"It's the ocean you are smelling, mistress. Salt water. Not good for the likes of you, I'll wager."

"I'll make do."

The woman was clad in a long diaphanous gown, the edges torn and tattered. They floated through the water as she swam back and forth at the surface.

Voices rose outside the wagon. A grunt and a thump. Shouting. The sound of feet on the steps outside.

The woman in the tank hissed as the door was thrown wide.

The clouds must have broken. Bright sunshine flooded the space, and Darkness was momentarily blinded.

His nose was filled with cooked sugar and cloying vanilla.

Sweetness and memory and gut-turning sadness. His nose was filled with *her*.

"Saints and sinners. What is this?" The voice was like a whisper from the past. One that should have been silent and dead lifetimes ago.

Darkness stepped between the woman in the tank and the woman in the doorway. He rubbed the light from his eyes and choked out a sound he couldn't remember ever making in all of his many many years.

"Bronwen? How?"

The newcomer pulled her eyes from the tank and tilted her head, something like confused recognition dancing in her eyes.

It had been ages since Darkness had a heart that was whole. Ages since he'd loved a woman with everything within him. Ages since he'd believed he could be more than just The Witch's son. And ages since that same woman had crushed his offered heart beneath the heel of her boot.

Standing in the flickering lantern light of the carnival wagon, he felt what was left of his heart leap to his throat right before it was ripped out completely when the only person he had truly ever loved looked at him and asked, "I'm sorry. Do I know you?"

Six

BEFORE

Elwell & Sons was in trouble. Bronwen knew it. Her father knew it. Enid and every other member of the troupe knew it.

None of them, however, spoke of it.

Not until that morning. The morning Bronwen approached her father with the empty tin box.

"Where's it gone, Da?"

"Where's what gone?"

"Don't play daft, Da. It doesn't suit you." She shook the box at him, the lack of jangling coins more damning than anything she could have spoken.

Alfie Elwell ran a dirt-smudged hand over his face. It left a mark on the tip of his nose.

"It's not worth fretting over. Money's been a bit tight just now, that's all."

"Tight, yes. Gone, no."

Her father didn't say anything. Didn't even look sheepish.

"There were coins enough in here yesterday, Da. I counted them myself. Coins meant for wages today."

He didn't speak as he massaged at the back of his neck, no doubt smudging dirt there as well.

"Da?"

He chewed his lower lip then spoke. "The crowd should be a good one tonight. I can feel it. Tell the crew we'll make good with them as soon as the tents are down."

Her stomach fell. She'd get no explanation then. It was left to her to calm the troupe and make them a promise she wasn't certain she'd be able to keep. Enid was no help—terrible as she was at managing anything other than a tight rope and a list of suitors—and despite the name, there were no sons to speak of.

Elwell & Daughters just didn't hold the same punch when it came down to it.

So that night, before the gates dropped, Bronwen handed out excuses rather than payroll. She was met with grumbling for the most part, but she didn't miss the few angry glares she received.

"I know it isn't what you all deserve, but if we can just get through the night, I'll see if I can't get us a day or two off before we head out," she said.

"What good's a day off if we've no money to enjoy it with, Bron? This keeps up, and some of us'll find it necessary to move on, aye?" Kerb was a whiz of pitch man, and they couldn't afford to lose him.

She didn't think he'd go—he like so many of the fellas lived for the show. And like just as many, he was a tad sweet on Enid. But he'd threaten it for certain, if for no other reason than to make a point.

"I'm confident that won't be necessary. The crowd's bound to be bonny. I can feel it. Just bring your tins directly to the sweets wagon tonight." The idea of cutting her father out of the collection felt treasonous, but the idea of him gambling away their pay and any chance of keeping the troupe together was somehow even worse. She'd keep the collection, pay out the wages, and hide away the rest. As much as she loved him, she wasn't above doing whatever she could to keep them going.

"All right then." She dusted her hands on her apron. "We've a show to put on. Let's get to it."

The group dispersed, taking their sour looks and frustrated sighs with them.

"How bad is it, Bronwen?" CJ stood arms crossed, leaning against the wood railing that blocked the carnival's entrance.

He was tall and wiry and, like Kerb, had a gift for this life. With his fantastic charisma, it didn't matter what attraction he was running, it always did well. He'd learned a lot from Alfie, but some things just couldn't be taught.

"Not good."

"They wouldn't have been happy, but they'd be a little less brittle if you gave them at least half a wage."

"I'm not daft. What's your point?"

He grimaced and shook his head. "But there isn't enough for even half, is there?"

"There is not."

CJ whistled through his teeth. "You're gonna need to do something."

"You think I'm not aware of that, CJ?" She bit the words out, irritated he'd found it necessary to confront her with it.

"Something big I mean."

"I'm all ears."

His tone didn't change, so she wasn't certain if he was joking or not when he said, "Something fey would be great."

She scoffed. "The fey are just stories."

"Don't be so sure. There's magic everywhere."

"I'm not wasting my time entertaining fantasies. I need

something solid now. Tonight would be great, but I'll settle for soon." She was growing oh so weary of this conversation. They both had work to do. She her confections and CJ the running of the tent of curiosities.

"You need an attraction that will not only draw them in but will also loosen their purse strings. Something no one else has got." He walked over and put his hands on her shoulders, forcing her to meet his gaze. "It's the only way to get the old man out of his debts."

"And where precisely am I to find this one of a kind, magical, nonexistent attraction?"

"I don't know, Bron. But if you don't, the show won't last the season."

The troupe made good on their promise, and Bronwen, thankfully, was able to make good on hers. The crowd wasn't overly impressive, but it was decent, and the coins brought in at the close of the night ended up with her rather than her father.

In the wee hours of the following morning, she counted out the wages, and after the stakes had been pulled and all but the living wagons loaded, she gave everyone the next day off. They each had just under twenty-four hours to do with as they pleased before the last of their camp was loaded onto the wagons and the group would pull out for the next stop on the circuit.

During the time she'd collected and redistributed the money and the time she helped tear down and pack up, she hadn't seen her father.

In fact, after doing his bit to draw the initial patrons to the gates with his flashy chatter and promises of wonders untold, he'd melted into the night and the hectic comings and goings of the carnival. He hadn't even been in the big top. Instead, he'd given over the MC duties to Rocky.

Alfie had always had a wonderful voice, just the right tone to capture hearts and imaginations. It was his gift as a show-man. He might not be the one walking the wire or spitting fire, but he sure made people want to hand over their coins to witness such things.

Bronwen wasn't surprised he didn't come to ask her why the troupe gave her the night's profits. He already knew. He was staying out of the eye of everyone. That itself must have been difficult. He loved being in the center of things. She could have sought him out, but the look of failure she was sure she'd see on his face wasn't something she was ready to deal with.

She figured he'd be holed up somewhere. Hopefully he was skipping the cards for a night. If he wasn't, she had no idea what coins he was doing it with. The idea of him having another secret stash was too unbelievable. She elected not to think about what he might be using in place of coins. Perhaps she should have.

"Me and some of the girls are going to the city, Winnie. Why don't you come along?"

Bronwen waved her sister off. "You go on, Enid. I need a bit of quiet."

"A bit of quiet? You're not gonna find that around here."

Enid was right. A day off meant drinking and games and general shenanigans for many of the troupe. They'd be making fools of themselves in a matter of hours. The city however was twice as noisy and infinitely more odorous.

She told her sister as much before they parted ways.

Bronwen tried to settle in their wagon with a good book. When that didn't work, she picked up the embroidery she'd been working on for the past six months. Tiny yellow daffodils were slowly taking shape on the edge of a swath of linen she intended to one day be a pillowcase. After one needle prick to her fingertip too many, she set the cloth down with a huff. Her mind kept returning to the conversation with CJ. As much as she hated to admit it, he was right. They needed an attraction to wow the masses. Something to draw them in from all over the countryside, not just the small towns and villages they set up in. Something to give Elwell & Sons the name recognition it needed if they were going to survive. Tasty treats, acts of daring, games of chance, and all the other standard carnival mystique could be found just as easily amongst the two or three competing groups.

She knew what she needed but had no idea where to find it.

A loud whooping erupted from outside, further snagging her attention. It was followed by the sound of glass toppling and then another round of raucous laughter.

With a sigh, she pulled the curtain and took in a group of the showmen running pell-mell through the campsite. To the man, they were half clad and all drunk.

As much as she hated to admit it, she probably should have gone along with her sister and the others to the city. She'd find no calm solitude in the camp. She needed to get away and find a quiet spot to be alone with her thoughts.

She recalled a small copse of trees following a brook just a ways back from their site.

Snagging an apple from the table by her bed, she headed out the door and away from the voices ringing between the wagons. It didn't take long for the sound of burbling water to reach her, and within minutes she found her way to the little stream with its moss-covered banks on either side. Birdsong and the buzz of insects mingled with the flowing water, creating a soothing melody. She had to fight the urge to lie down and take a nap.

Unfortunately, it was no time for napping. She needed to come up with a decent plan sooner rather than later.

What would bring in the most coins? If she were a spectator, what would she want to see? What would she pay *extra* to see? A magician? A sword swallower? A crone draped in secrets ready to spill her deepest desires?

No, she'd want something more. Something fantastic. A creature of some ilk. A maiden half bird and half woman. A pixie with wings of fire. A devilishly handsome man who could genuinely levitate or potions that allowed the patrons to smell colors and see songs.

Any of it would do, but none of it actually existed. Fey stories weren't real. Everyone with any sense knew it. And even if they were, how would she convince someone to join the carnival? The pay was reasonable but the travel was rough.

So how to find someone who could create the illusion? Perhaps a talented seamstress to conjure creatures from fabric and feathers? And once that problem was solved, there still remained the issue of her father. This was his show, but if he couldn't keep his demons at bay, what was the point of bringing in more for him to lose?

The sun was beginning to fall behind the trees, but still Bronwen couldn't bring herself to abandon her sanctuary. If she stayed long enough, maybe, just maybe, a solution would find its way into her thoughts and all of her troubles would disappear. She puffed out her cheeks and blew out a long breath. Talk about fey stories.

"Too pretty a face to fill it with such solicitude."

Bronwen's head snapped up, and she twisted, rising to her knees to face the trees at her back. Though her gaze searched the space, there was no sign of the owner of the deep and resonant voice.

"Ahhh. And now another sort of disquiet fills the lovely countenance."

A shiver raced up her spine. The voice was directly before her, but no body could be seen.

"Who's there?" She pushed to her feet. "Show yourself, sir."

"Sir?" She could hear the laugh in the rich lush voice. "You know me not well enough for the title."

She strained her eyes and tilted her head. She was sure he was just there, beneath the trees, not a dozen paces away. Yet all she could make out were the shadowy limbs of the alder and poplar. Shadows upon shadows upon shadows.

"Not worth the effort. I assure you." His tone was teasing but with a slice of menace she didn't care for.

Oh, she was a careless fool. So wrapped up in her worries that she'd wandered off without telling a soul where she'd be. Anything could happen in the dark of the forest.

She stepped to the side and glanced at the path she'd taken to get there. How quick could she be?

"And now I've gone and frightened you. No need, my little sweet. That's what you smell of. Sweets and bonbons and biscuits and cakes. Can we agree, sweetness?"

His wording was ever so slightly odd, but his voice was near to mesmerizing. Not overly deep, but strong and pleasant.

"I'm not sure what you're asking me. Perhaps if you'd show yourself it might be discussed."

She didn't really want to discuss anything. But if she knew where he was, her possibility of escape was higher.

"Perhaps. Another time." If it was possible, the shadows grew thicker still. "For now, I'll stay where I am and you may go back to your butter and syrup and spices. I sense that is what you wish. Or . . . I can be an ear for your worries."

"I've no worries to share with a man I can't see. You lurk there, in the shadows, and ask that I converse?"

"Have you someone better with which to share time?"

"I do." It wasn't strictly true, but she wasn't going to tell a disembodied voice as much. Let him think there was someone waiting for her return.

He chuckled low. A mock. Her temper rose.

"You don't believe me?"

"It makes not a difference if I do or I do not."

"Then why do you laugh?"

"I have my reasons."

"And you'll not share them."

"Why would I share my reasons if you won't share your woes?"

This was getting absurd. Long past absurd really. Bronwen had better things to do with her time. Like figure out how to save the carnival from her father's folly.

"You've taken enough of my time today, sir."

"Again with sir. It will not do. If you must name me something, name me Darkness."

A shudder ran through her at his words. It began at the base of her neck and traveled the length of her body to each and every finger and toe. The skin on her scalp tingled, and her heart increased its tempo. It wasn't an altogether unpleasant sensation, and that made her even more ill at ease.

"Darkness?" Her voice wasn't nearly as strong as she'd like.

"Aye." There was no teasing in that one word. It was low and dark and commanding.

Her voice was tremulous when she replied. "You've taken enough of my time today, Darkness."

"Not possible I'm afraid. I could never capture time enough with a lass who smells like decadence itself." His voice was more enticing than it ought to be.

She swallowed and stepped back.

"Another time then," he said.

She opened her mouth to respond, but no words came.

And then he was gone.

She didn't see him leave. But why should she? She hadn't seen him at all during their interaction. She knew, however, the moment he vanished. The shadows lifted and where she was sure he'd been standing was now only a thick grouping of trees, the leaves dappled with fading evening light.

❦

"Someone was having a go with you, that's all." Enid adjusted the new hair comb she'd returned with from the city while she studied herself in the looking glass. "Darkness?" She snorted a laugh. "It's not very original now, is it?"

"How do you mean?" Bronwen didn't think her sister would discount things so easily if she'd only been there. She could still feel the odd mix of trepidation and curiosity the man's voice conjured, and for the first time she wondered if this was anything like the thrill-seeking Enid looked for when she was soaring over a crowd.

"Well, it's the old nanny story, isn't it? Dub or Dutch or whatever the names were. I don't recall. But you know? The brothers. One was evil and another wicked or something, and the third was darkness."

Now that Enid said it, Bronwen recalled bits of the story. "The witch's sons. Yes. You're right."

"Well, so . . . it was probably just one of the lads. They followed you down there and were having a go at you. You should have come with me to the city like I suggested."

"Maybe." Bronwen didn't think it was any of the men from the troupe. Even if they were somehow able to disguise their voices, she didn't know any of them with a talent for illusion who would render the man unseen to her eye. If they did, perhaps Elwell & Sons would have larger crowds.

"At any rate, the city was divine. I wish Da would rent out a theater and make this a real show. We could live in the rafters and shop in the streets. Once people realized how exceptional the show is, we'd become known through the city and be invited to the poshest parties and dress in silks and have an endless line of suitors ready to make us offers. Which we would of course refuse, because why settle with just one?" Enid lay back and stared up at the ceiling, daydreams dancing in her eyes while Bronwen busied herself tiding up the space.

"All well and good for the death-defying Enid Elwell and her highwire act, but what of my confections or the curiosities? The fortune booths and the bits that don't exactly meet the high society standards?"

"Oh, I'm sure that could be figured out. And you don't need to only sell confections, Bronwen. Your talents could lie elsewhere. You just need to figure them out."

That stung just a tad.

"But I like making candies and cakes."

Without raising her body, Enid adjusted her head and looked at Bronwen. "No one is saying you couldn't still do that. But you've got to dream bigger, Winnie.

"My dreams are just the size they ought to be, thank you." Bronwen shoved a loose pair of stockings into the top bureau drawer.

"And what size is that?"

"The size that keeps this troupe together and food in our bellies."

Enid sat up quickly, hands resting on the edge of her bunk as she leaned forward. "That's it? Nothing more than keeping us alive? What about boys at your feet and enough coins to buy whatever your heart desires?"

"First of all, I've no interest in *boys*. We've enough *boys* here. Even the ones twice my age. I think a man would be preferable. One who doesn't need watching after or scolding or direction to get things done. An actual partner to help share my burdens." *I can be an ear for your worries.* She slammed the drawer shut. "And secondly, I don't quite have your taste for the finer things. Give me a good kettle and a cozy bed and—"

"That man to keep it warm," Enid interrupted.

Bronwen rolled her eyes. "And I will be happy. But you're right about one thing."

"I'm right about a lot of things, but go on."

"It would be nice not to worry over the finances every moment of every day." Bronwen sighed and sat down next to her sister. She barely remembered their mother, but part of Bronwen thought maybe things would be different if she'd still been around.

"You shouldn't be worried about that at all, Winnie. Da's got to know that."

"I'm not saying he doesn't," Bronwen said.

"It's not right. It's not Bronwen & Sons."

"Technically I am still an Elwell. And so are you."

"Yes, but if you hadn't noticed, neither of us are 'sons.' I've no wish to be in charge. You know that."

"I do." Bronwen *did* know it. She didn't really want to be in charge either, but someone had to keep things afloat. "But you can't really think moving to a fixed theater in the city would solve that problem, do you?"

"If we got popular enough, we could hire a manager. Someone who knows how to manage. The simple fact is no one with those sorts of credentials wants to be living out of tents and wagons."

Bronwen stilled and in a small voice asked what she'd been wondering about for some time. "Are you thinking of leaving, Enid?"

"Leaving? The troupe? Oh, Winnie. No." Enid scooted

over and wrapped Bronwen in a tight hug. "This is my home. And more than that, *you* are my home. But that doesn't mean I'll give up on my dreams so easily. And neither should you. Dream big, Winnie. Dream of more than a man and more than enough to keep us afloat. Dream big for yourself. No one else is gonna do it for you."

Seven

❧

Bronwen woke with a start, the dream still so vivid in her mind.

Dream big, Winnie.

A dream but not a dream. It felt more like a memory. A confusing memory to be sure.

Everything about it was just a bit off. Not unlike when she'd woken to find herself younger than she ought to be. In the dream memory, there hadn't been a train to move them from site to site and all of her clothing was considerably out of fashion. Enid's too and that would never happen.

She was a confectioner for Colger & Sons—not Elwell & Sons.

But she *had* been. She knew that now.

Her father had run the carnival. This carnival—give or take. Some of the faces and the names still remained, she remembered that much. *Her father had run the carnival.* But at some point it had fallen to her to keep it afloat. She had struggled. She knew that now. But when had it failed? When had CJ taken over? That was still a blank.

And in her memory, there hadn't been a steam engine,

65

only wagons. There hadn't been the same quality of costumes. Not even the same attractions. Everything had been antiquated and somewhat old-fashioned. It contributed to the dreamlike quality that confused her.

What was more, she remembered that day by the creek. The voice that had entranced and terrified her. Darkness he'd called himself.

While she couldn't recall anything further, not his face or even if she'd seen him again, she remembered his voice.

A voice that sounded suspiciously similar to the man's who'd been inside that horrible wagon with the girl in the tank.

That man she remembered well. He was certainly no dream or foggy figment of her imagination.

He was tall and dark and had a face born of her wildest dreams. Alabaster skin, hair and eyes the pitch of midnight.

And he'd known her name. How had he known her name?

She hadn't had the chance to ask. As soon as he'd spoken to her, Enid and Lucy had rushed into the wagon, several other girls following close behind and CJ at the door barking orders.

Bronwen had been so taken aback by the entire scene she'd stood there nearly frozen while her sister rushed to the tanks and threw a rope around the woman's neck. With a sharp jerk, Enid pulled the dark-haired beauty to one side of the tank and held her pinned there while Lucy and two other sturdy young women—whose names escaped Bronwen—grabbed the long hook-ended poles they trained with on the trapeze. They used the poles to lift the bodies—dead bodies—from the bottom of the tank and over the side. She flinched at the wet thunks they made as they hit the floor, and then she was spinning.

Or the wagon was spinning. Spinning and growing smaller and darker and voices and sounds were far away and then the dark-haired man was calling her name and Enid was hissing the word "you" at someone and then there was nothing but black as she fell to the floor.

She'd obviously passed out and woken in her bed with no idea how she'd gotten there and no idea why under all the stars in the heavens there was a woman in a tank in the center of the carnival.

Judging by the light filtering in, it wasn't quite nightfall, but the sounds of the carnival were growing louder. She hadn't finished the list of treats she'd needed, but at this point she didn't care.

Something unsavory was happening in the space around her, and vats of sugar and honey weren't going to sweeten it no matter how she wished they would. It was maddening, this confusion. She needed to understand her life.

A knock came at the door.

It likely wasn't Enid knocking, however. Not only would her sister just barge in, but if the sun was going down, she'd be in the big top getting dressed and applying her makeup or already warming up for her show.

The knock came again.

"Ah, just a moment."

Bronwen stood and put on a calm face. Whoever it was didn't need to know how distraught she was. Even Enid—her Enid—had played a part in that horrific scene.

She had no doubt the woman was being held against her will. The rope around her neck and the one binding her in the water were proof of it. But clearly she was dangerous. The two dead men were proof of that. Had Bronwen herself been aware of the reason for it? She didn't think so. As much as her past was a mystery, she was sure she knew herself well enough not to go along with something so heinous.

Taking a deep breath, she steeled herself and opened the door.

She startled. CJ was dressed in his showman's finest. Tailored suit, silk cravat, and crisp top hat included. They contrasted severely with his blackened eye and split lower lip. "May I come in?"

"Oh, CJ. What happened?"

Then another memory. A tall white-haired man, with both brutality and glee in his eyes. He'd been taking on half the troupe when Bronwen—drawn by the sounds of wailing and cries, Tommy close behind—arrived and headed into the wagon. She hadn't taken any care to look at CJ in all the excitement, but he must have been injured more than she'd realized.

And Tommy. She hoped he was all right. It would be just like him to try to take on anyone threatening CJ.

CJ dipped his head forward toward the entrance.

"Yes. Yes, of course. Come in."

She hadn't lit the lamp, and whoever had brought her back here hadn't either. She picked up a box of matches, but CJ stopped her. "Don't bother. This won't take long and you've got sweets to sell."

"All right then." She set down the box.

"I understand what you saw today was distressing to you, but I never suspected it would be quite *so* distressing." He certainly didn't sound sorry for causing her distress.

"A woman tied in a tank. I'm fairly sure most folks would take it as a bit of a shock."

"Most people maybe. But, Bronwen, *we* are not most people. *We* are showmen. We specialize in the fantastical, do we not?"

"I'm not certain what is so fantastical about holding a helpless person against their will."

"Helpless." He scoffed. Beyond the damage to his face, Bronwen saw a deeper fatigue. He wasn't a young man, but in the past days, he'd seemed to age even more. "Try telling that to Ty and Rocky."

The dead men in the tank. Guilt crashed through her. She'd known those men, and rather than grieving their loss, she'd been focused on the girl who must have killed them.

"I assure you she is not *helpless*. She is a water maiden, and she is going to make this carnival lots and lots of money."

A rusalka? It couldn't be. Even whispers of the water maidens were rare, if they were to be believed at all. Beautiful young women who lured men to the rivers just to watch them drown, all to assuage their broken hearts. Even if the fey were making themselves known of late, it was a rare form of magic to possess and, if the stories were to be believed, a dark magic —born of pain and misery and shame. Magic strong enough and dark enough to turn happy and hale young women into monsters.

Moreover, what good was that to the carnival?

"And how do you propose she do that? What sort of show do you expect her to put on?" Water maidens weren't known to possess anything more than their murderous voices. Was CJ planning to kill an audience member each night? It seemed unlikely.

"I haven't gotten that far yet. I only just stumbled upon the opportunity for her employ. I'll think of something once I get her to trust me."

Employ. That was a stretch. Not many people found captivity to be a lucrative career.

"But that aside," CJ continued, "I wouldn't expect that reaction from you. So tell me, Bronwen, was it the new addition to our troupe that affected you so, or was it him?"

"Him?"

CJ stepped toward her, hands balled at his sides. "Don't play daft with me. We've known each other far too long for that."

"You're the one being daft, CJ. In case you don't recall, my brain is still quite foggy, and as you so kindly told me, you aren't willing to explain things. It makes sense that I wouldn't remember every member of the troupe."

"That man is no member of this troupe. It will all come back, and when it does you'll understand. Until then, remember this. If Darkness or any other vile member of his family steps foot inside these grounds again, I *will* kill him."

Bronwen flinched back as if slapped. *If you must name me something, name me Darkness.* It was him, but that wasn't the only thing that bothered her.

CJ had never been the violent sort, and it shocked her to hear him make the threat. It would have been laughable in other circumstances. Clearly the elderly man before her was no match for the man she'd seen by that tank. As for his family, she could only assume he meant the striking man with the white flowing hair and the gleeful eyes. Judging by CJ's face, it was clear who'd come out on top in that match earlier.

By the way he'd said it, cold and sure and knowingly, Bronwen could tell CJ meant it as no idle threat.

"Do we understand one another?"

She nodded.

He smiled, all the charm and good humor returning to his face. "Good. Now let's go put on a show."

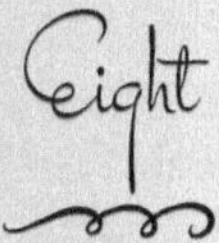

Eight

"Can we do things my way this time?"

Moonlight filtered down through the trees where Darkness and Violence stood watching the line of patrons entering the carnival.

"I suppose, Dub. But my way was fun, aye?"

"Fun for you, perhaps. I think the showmen might disagree."

"They loved it as much as I did. Trust me. I know what lurks in the hearts of men."

Darkness snorted and ran a hand over his face. "We shouldn't have left her."

"Her?" Violence slung an arm over his brother's shoulder. "And which her are we referring to?"

Darkness shoved Violence off. "I told you. There was a rusalka in that tank."

"Yes, yes. So you've said. I think in these parts they prefer the term water maiden, but no matter. Who else was in that wagon, Dub?" He crossed his hands over his chest and studied his brother. "When you emerged, it was as if you'd seen a ghost, brother. And we both know it wasn't that old withered prune nor the vicious lovely in the tank who had you so upset."

Violence was right. The sight of Bronwen had been like seeing a ghost. There was no earthly way the woman could have been his Bronwen. His Bronwen had to be decades in her grave by now.

But she'd looked just as she had the last time he'd seen her. Young and lovely and full of the infectious good nature and vitality he'd been so drawn to lifetimes ago. And she'd smelled the same too. Sugar and cream. Vanilla and apples ripe from the orchard.

"There was no one else." He'd be damned for a fool to share any of that with either of his brothers.

"Mmm-hmm." Violence nodded with false solemnity. "Well then, perhaps it was the old prune after all."

The old prune had seemed familiar as well, but Darkness couldn't place him, and then there was the other young woman. She'd certainly known who he was. And he'd known her. The old man called for a girl named Enid. That had been the name of Bronwen's sister.

He'd uttered Bronwen's name and she'd looked at him and he'd been so sure it was her, but then . . . *I'm sorry, but do I know you?*

She hadn't recognized him. At all.

But Enid had. And his head was reeling with what it meant that not only was Bronwen in that wagon, but so was Enid. And that knowledge left him just as shaken. If this was his chance to right things, why then was Enid also here in this time? She too should have been long in the ground.

There were dark days in his past when he'd hated Bronwen's sister. Not because of any one insult. Not because she had an unaffable character. Not because she was a snob or a murderer or any other of a number of things he detested. He hated her for one simple reason. She had the one thing he never could. Every day of her life with Bronwen.

Or at least he presumed she had.

He honestly had not a clue what had transpired in the years since he'd last seen them.

It couldn't be them.

His mind was getting tricky again. He'd do well to remember it.

"It hurts you to admit I am right. I understand. Being bested by an old man. Wait til Dother hears."

Darkness knew his brother was baiting him. It had always been like this. Ever since the beginning. Darkness and Violence and Evil. Each other's best friends and worst enemies. He supposed all brothers were like that to a certain extent. Violence would rub at him until he gave in and told him what he wanted to know. Now however wasn't the time for that particular conversation, so he kept his tongue tight behind his lips.

"Now, what does your way of doing things entail?" Violence asked, letting go of the morsel.

"My head says that way." Darkness pointed.

Violence looked to the carnival entrance, merriment sparkling in his icy eyes. "Through the front? They'll be wary after this afternoon. Looking for us." Violence's smile grew. "It sounds perfect."

"Not the line." Darkness didn't share that he'd done the very thing just days ago—slipping in as a patron. But his brother was right. After the events of earlier that day, the showmen were apt to be looking for trouble. And while he was sure they could mitigate any unpleasantness, he'd rather not have to deal with such things. "The opening. To the far side."

Just beyond the tent that served as a gateway to the carnival, a gap could be seen. To the other side of the gap was a line of wooden posts that were strung through with rope adorned with brightly colored flags. It was a ridiculous barrier. The showmen clearly relied on the good nature of the folk in this part of the world. Anyone wanting to slip under would have no trouble at all. Most nights, an extra hand likely wandered back and forth, keeping watch for the occasional troublemaker attempting to step inside without paying. If they were patrolling that night, Darkness was confident he could keep from being seen.

Just to the other side of the flimsy marker, the back ends of several stalls opened along the grassy alley. He wasn't sure which attractions lay that way. Not the wagon with the river maiden and not the confectionary. Those were buried farther in.

"And once we are inside?"

Darkness didn't look at Violence as he said, "Once I'm inside, I'll head for the wagon."

Violence tsked. "Now, brother. If I didn't know better, I'd say that sounds as if you plan to leave me out of this little mission."

"Not leave you out exactly."

"So how *exactly* will I be involved?" Violence mused.

"You'll be involved by heading back to the cottage and collecting Mother. I think she needs to be here when I free the water maiden. The girl's bound to be a lot to handle."

"All the more reason for me to join you."

"All the more reason to have the witch Carman here to help sooth her," Darkness corrected.

"Fine. Then I'll fetch the lass and you fetch Mother."

"No debate to be had, brother. I've already spoken to the rusalka. Knows me and I her. It'll be quicker and hopefully quieter for me to go."

"And yet you send me to fetch Mother under the auspices of soothing the girl. Pick your path. Can't have it both ways."

"Time is wasting," Darkness said. "I will slip in with the shadows. You would barrel in there fists raised. It makes sense. This you know."

"Oh, aye. I know. Just like to rile you a bit before I'm off."

Darkness cursed and Violence smiled. "I'll see you in a wee bit."

Violence jogged off into the trees, and Darkness pulled his shadows close then slipped in through the gap near at the ropes.

Just as it had several nights earlier, the music of the carnival swept over him, the cacophony of notes and melody buoying him as he entered the carnival grounds. Keeping the gloom tight to his body, he sidled along the edge of the entrance tent. He could hear the ticket taker inside the canvas grumbling to a group of patrons but couldn't make out the words.

As suspected, not one but two men walked along the row of stalls and tents in the space between the rope barrier and field beyond. Darkness stayed where he was, not wanting the movement of even his shadows to draw their attention. If he'd have been running the show, he might have had a word with the pair, for they seemed much more interested in each and every pretty girl to pass on both sides of the rope than on anything else. More the better for Darkness and his quest.

Once they were halfway down the row, Darkness took his opportunity. With his natural speed and unnatural power to command the night around him, he was able to move past the entrance and further into the innumerable diversions beyond.

He turned a corner at the house of frights and came upon a small booth filled with teacups and glass bottles of varying sizes. A group of young girls were attempting to land a small copper on one of the vessels, the prize for which was a small trinket. None of the girls was having much success.

He looked away from the amusement in time to avoid

colliding face first with a clown of sorts. Or, more accurately, chest first as her head barely made it past his sternum. The error was completely his own as he was the one masked in shadow.

The woman was dressed in a motley assortment of kerchiefs, all in various shades of orange and green. They assembled a garment fit for a babydoll if said babydoll had escaped from the asylum. It was near painful to look at, much too short, revealing garish puce knickers and at the same time overly voluminous. Her face was painted a chalky white with overly exaggerated eyelashes and lips that gave the impression of both a strumpet and a ghoul. It would have made quite the mess of his attire had he not avoided the run-in. She was carrying a basket overfilled with rose petals she flung into the air haphazardly.

Although Darkness pulled back in time to save himself from a very unfortunate collision and didn't think the clown saw him, she must have sensed a disturbance of some sort. With an exaggerated frown, she clutched the basket of petals to her bosom and hurried off in the opposite direction.

He moved to the side and skirted the same group of copper-tossing girls as they chased after the clown, giggling. The aisle was filling with more and more patrons as the evening wore on. Darkness was surprised to note he recognized many of them.

Recently his mother had elected to stay in the area of Feyport, not something any of them had expected. For more years than he could count, they had been on the move, much like the carnivals, moving from spot to spot on an endless journey through the land. While he didn't strictly live with his mother, he was always near, should she have a task for him. The same was true of both Dother and Dain, but they were better at staying hidden until such a time as they were needed.

Because Darkness was restless, he found himself watching the denizens of Feyport.

He'd learned the young and the old. Studied the ones marked with fey magic and had even had conversations with them on occasion.

Now he saw many of them. And while he remained hidden, he was certain if he were to show himself, it wouldn't be the folks of Feyport who would have a problem with him at the fair. They might startle at the sight, but they wouldn't do anything too foolish. Either way, it mattered little. His plan was to stay deeply immersed in gloom and grey until absolutely necessary. If luck and the night were on his side, that might mean getting through the cavalcade of attractions and their various showmen, to the river bottom wagon, freeing the water maiden without her fruitless attempts on his life, and back out again, all without being seen by a single member of the troupe.

Darkness should have known that while the night was his closest confidant, luck remained, as ever, his enemy.

He was midway through the grounds, keeping to the back side of a row of stalls, when he heard the carousel's staccato melody. Given how it had affected him previously and now knowing twisted magic was afoot, he'd thought himself prepared for it. While he was able to keep from heading in the direction of the horrid thing, his feet still felt the slightest tug, and before he could right himself, he'd stepped out into the flow of foot traffic, nearly colliding with a round-faced woman and her equally round-faced child.

The woman, harried as she was, didn't notice Darkness, but the small boy did. The child stopped midstride and smiled up at him. Darkness did not smile back.

Two near misses in just as many minutes.

The music continued to play on, and strangely, it didn't

seem to affect the other patrons in any way. Meanwhile, Darkness had to concentrate to keep its hold from taking him over.

Curious.

With a little effort, he was able to place it to the back of his mind and step out of the line of foot traffic.

He was meant to be headed to the far south corner of the grounds where the water maiden's makeshift prison stood, but when he'd regained himself he cringed to see where he'd ended up. Right beside a bright pink and white striped wagon.

He was so close in fact, he could practically taste the salted caramel in the damp evening air. A small line had formed in front of the wagon—mostly children of various ages all angling for a tasty treat. But a fair number of adults were exclaiming over not just the simple candy floss and lollies, but over cleverly crafted chocolate confections, sugar mice, and any number of hand-sized pies, their crusts shiny in the twinkling lights.

His eyes drifted from the throng of patrons to the woman busily swapping coins for the delicacies. The wagon's side wall was flipped down to reveal a glass case filled with a variety of beautiful pastries, cakes, and candies. Behind the case a large hopper was filled with toffee-coated popping corn.

Just as brimming as the hopper, his memory was filled with the perfect combination of salty buttery sweet goodness. He remembered the first time they had met. She hadn't seen him, of course, but it hadn't made the encounter any less intriguing for him. She'd been so cutoff and reserved, weighed down as she was. He'd been so pleased as he'd gotten through those layers of woe to see the lovely soul beneath it all. He'd marveled at her really. So light and giving and just as enticing as the edible wonders she created.

But then it ended. And so had the light within his darkness.

No matter now. That was then.

A young man stood on one end of the opening, handing out confections after they'd been paid for, and next to him, taking orders and collecting coins was the most lovely girl under all the moon and stars. Her hair was pulled into a knot at the top of her head but it was the same thick honey blonde it had been that day by the creek. Her skin the same freckle-dusted peach and her eyes the same feather grey.

But even from this distance Darkness noted the lack of merriment in those soft eyes he'd loved all those long years ago. He wanted to know what had dimmed them, but after the lifetimes they'd spent apart, he supposed it could have been anything really.

And he reminded himself, it was no longer his concern to find out the cause. Bronwen herself had made that much abundantly clear the last time they'd spoken.

While he was curious about her apparent immortality, or at the very least magical longevity, he had no reason to think she'd tell him if he asked. Apparently she didn't even remember him. After all of it, even decades later, it still caused a gaping ache in his chest.

And yet he was so forgettable for her.

He'd offered her everything. Love. A life together. Even a lifeline to save her father's troupe, and she'd efficiently and effectively declined the offer. It was that last conversation he thought about as he turned to seek out his real business at the carnival that night.

He'd made it no more than a half dozen steps when he heard her.

"Wait."

He couldn't say when he'd dropped the cloak of gloom concealing himself, but clearly he had and she had seen him.

Not good. Not good. Who else had seen?

Blessed mother. His mind was no longer just tricky. It was

inept. If Dain or Dother had been there, he'd never hear the end of it.

"Please. Wait."

"Ah. Mistress." He smirked at Bronwen. If she didn't remember him, best to play along. "How may I assist?"

"Darkness, you can't be here. If he sees. . ."

"Oh, so you remember me now, mistress?"

"I . . . well, yes, but no. Not really." She worried at her lower lip and looked away from him.

His heart fell.

"I know we've met before. Or at least I think I remember meeting before. It doesn't matter now. You've got to leave. Please."

"But I've just gotten here. Wonders await, do they not?"

She looked over her shoulder and grabbed his elbow, pulling him to the side. Her eyes were near frantic as they flicked back and forth down the row of stalls.

The past notwithstanding, something in him cracked a bit to see her so distraught.

"Here now, mistress. Calm yourself." He gathered the night and cloaked them both. "This will do, will it not?"

"How did you do that? And why are you speaking like that?"

"And how am I speaking?" She must not remember him at all if the shadows took her by surprise.

"I don't know. In that odd cadence."

"Odd is it?" He smirked. "It's how I speak."

She shook her head. "Not all the time, it's not."

"And how would you know that?" He kept his voice low.

"I don't know. I just do. I don't remember exactly, but I'm sure of it. There's lots I don't remember."

He frowned. "I see."

"Do you? Then perhaps you can explain it to me."

"That would require a certain amount of trust, mistress.

And I'm not certain you'd like to trust me just now." Like river water over stones, the fairgoers moved around them, gliding away from the dark patch along the back of a tent. "Does the darkness not scare you?"

She looked around, now her turn to frown. "No, should it?"

It did once. At least that was the pretty lie she told.

He didn't tell her so.

"Mistress. I have business this night." He was in no mood for games upon games.

"That's what I'm trying to tell you." Her voice was louder than it ought to be, and he told her as much.

"The darkening doesn't damper the noise then?"

He shook his head. She truly did not remember. It hurt more than he cared for. "It does. But I am right here, mistress. No need to shout."

She winced, and try as he might, he couldn't help but feel a bit of guilt.

When she spoke next, she spoke just above a whisper and leaned in to him. "He's got men outside the water maiden's wagon. I don't know how you escaped earlier, and I don't know why you're a threat to him, but CJ means to have you killed should he see you here again. And you didn't answer me. How is it that we are cloaked in darkness?"

Again he refused to answer. It would be easier to explain how light danced on water or how bird song could soothe a broken heart.

How he had escaped however? That was just silly.

If she thought he and Violence couldn't extricate them-selves from a handful of showmen, well, she clearly did not remember him at all.

He wasn't sure what to make of it. Or of the fact that she so clearly worried at his safety now.

He vaguely recalled a man by that name from his time

with her before. This was getting to be a bit much. First Bronwen and then Enid. Now someone wishing him harm. Young when they had no right to be.

What were they then? There were only a handful of ways for a person to gain immortality after all. He liked none of them. He itched to ask her, but other mysteries were more pressing just then.

"CJ?" he asked.

"Colger. The proprietor. He told me earlier today."

"Told you what, mistress?"

"Saints and sinners. Stop calling me mistress. It's so . . . I don't know. Just please don't call me that."

"And if I don't call you mistress, than how should I name you?" It was on the tip of his tongue to use the old name he'd given her. He bit his tongue sharply to prevent it.

"Bronwen will do."

"It will indeed. Or should you prefer Ms. Elwell?"

"I don't recall sharing my last name with you."

"No? Perhaps not. Now what did this man tell you?"

"That should he find you or any of your family within the grounds, he would harm you." She worried at her lip with the confession.

"Harm me?"

"Well, kill you actually."

"Kill me?" He smiled.

"Or any of your family," she added. "I don't know why you're smiling."

"I see." He thanked the universe for sending Violence away earlier. He'd have enjoyed this conversation a bit too much.

"You've said that before. I wish you'd explain it to me. I have no idea why he reacted in such a way. It isn't like him. Or at least I don't believe it's like him."

"Interesting. As for your earlier question—of how I

escaped—quite a simple task. I melted into the shadows and then left of my own accord. My safety should not concern you so. It was easy enough to slip away earlier and it will be easier yet to do it now. Sadly, in the rush I was unprepared to do what need be done. Hence my return this evening."

"What need be done? I wish you'd speak plainly." He could see the frustration in her eyes and sensed it wasn't solely with him.

"And if I were to tell you my plans plainly, I suppose you'd run to your proprietor and share them?"

She opened her mouth to reply quickly but paused. "Only if you were planning to harm someone."

"I've no such plans. The opposite in fact."

She stepped ever so slightly back and looked up into his eyes, understanding drawing on her face. "The water maiden."

"Perchance."

"I don't know why he has her, nor what he plans to do, but I can tell you, she is safe tonight. I can't say the same for you, if you try to free her."

He didn't believe anyone could promise the rusalka's safety, least of all the delicate little candy maker. "Then I suppose we shall see."

"Please. Darkness. I don't know how we are connected, but I know there must be something. If ever there was a time you trusted me, I ask that you think on that now. I won't let harm come to her while she is within the troupe. If you can wait, I'd like to help you free her. But tonight isn't the night."

"I did trust you once." His voice was quieter still, lost in all that was between them, whether she remembered it or not.

"And you can't do it again?"

The question snapped him back. "Tricky that answer."

"All right then. As much as that stings, I suppose it's fair." It was so like her, to take what he said and be earnestly honest with her reply. He wanted to hug her to him. He wanted to turn around and never look back.

"It needs to be soon. No one, magical or otherwise, should be held against their choice," he said.

She nodded. "I agree. I can slip away tomorrow. We can work out a plan."

"Tomorrow."

"You'll leave now? Without being seen?"

"My word on it, mistr— Bronwen."

She sighed and the tension left her shoulders. "Good. I've got to get back to the wagon. Tommy is a wonderful lad, but not everyone is as patient with him as they ought to be."

He nodded and stepped back. As he pulled the gloom with him, he couldn't help but marvel at how she glowed in the carnival lights.

"A favor before I go?"

She stared into the shadows, directly at him, as if her eyes alone could penetrate the darkness. "Yes?"

"When tomorrow we meet, I'd find a bit of joy in a sweet." It was a test of sorts. One he wasn't sure he wanted her to pass.

She smiled brightly. "Absolutely. I recommend the cherry-lime bonbons. They're magical."

And with those words, he felt the barest spark of light in his soul.

Nine

"Oh, dear boy. I'm rather relieved you got here before I ventured out. I thought you had things in hand."

"My apologies, Mother." Darkness dipped his head to Carman. "There was an unexpected twist of events."

"I told you I should have gone in with you."

Darkness glared at his brother.

"A group of showmen have you frightened. Wait til I tell Dother." Violence was enjoying himself entirely too much.

"So the poor dear remains?" Carman asked.

"She does. I believe she will remain unharmed for the time."

"And why would you believe that?" She tapped her chin.

"I was given a certain assurance," Darkness answered.

"By whom?"

"It was a friend. Someone I met some time ago." There was no doubt now it was his Bronwen. He had no idea how or why, but it *was* her.

"And this friend can be trusted?"

Could she? He didn't know. "I hold hope with me, yes."

"Interesting." Carman reclined in the chair she occupied in the small front room of her cottage near Feyport.

Darkness had left immediately after his exit from the carnival to intercept Violence and his mother. It wouldn't do to have them arrive when he wasn't there, water maiden in hand. The witch wouldn't be angered per se, but neither would she be happy.

Carman did things on her own terms. Often those terms were a mystery to everyone but her. Evil, Violence, and Darkness included. Her sons had learned long ago not to question it, even if her instructions were often murky or absurd. The very fact that she had the three with her, at her call, always and forever, was in and of itself quite curious.

Darkness often wondered how exactly the three of them came into being. It was possible they'd been born from her just as any other child born into the world and then she'd worked her magic on their young bodies to make them what they were today. Or perhaps she conjured them directly from the earth and the air, water, and fire. Darkness wondered, but he did not ask. None of the brothers did. Whether from disinterest or fear he wasn't sure. Darkness didn't even know which of them was the eldest, only that they always had been together. He simply took them as his family and went on with it. Not a typical family true, but his family nonetheless.

And so he was happy he'd intercepted them lest she devise some other more interesting plan to retrieve the girl from the tank.

Then there was the charm.

"Did you tell her the other bit?" he asked Violence.

His brother looked at him with mild disgust. "Do you think me the same fool as you? Of course I did."

"The suspense of seeing it for myself is most intoxicating, Dub." The look on her face was akin to a child staring at a mountain of sweets wrapped in beautiful paper and twine—

hungry, excited, and just a bit fearful of the belly ache they were sure to experience at the end.

"Now, on to the business at hand." Gone was the hungry excitement, to be replaced by the keen-eyed cleverness he knew so well. "We have three tasks as I see them. Find this menacing magic and release the maiden from her tank."

He was almost afraid to ask. "And the third?"

"Make these unfortunate showmen see the error of their ways."

Darkness swallowed but showed no other outward sign of his distress. He needed to know how it was Bronwen and her friends were still walking the earth but wasn't quite ready to share that bit with his family.

"Now, I want you both to understand, this has nothing to do with your capabilities." She grabbed Violence's hand and patted it as he frowned down at her. "But I've got someone in mind to assist us."

"We don't need assistance," Violence said.

"Of course you don't. But I have been itching to see what our darling selkie is capable of. This is the perfect test, don't you think?"

Violence groaned audibly. "I'd rather carve my eye out with a rusted spoon than listen to that arrogant seal."

Carman had a way of collecting fey and regular folk alike. Recently, she'd traded a favor with a selkie. He got what he needed and Carman got him in a sense.

"Well, your eyes are much too mesmerizing for that, so you'll just need to make due."

Darkness didn't quite share his brother's disdain for Declan. He'd thought the selkie had made a fairly smart deal. In exchange for mending his broken magic, he'd agreed to give up his tie to the sea. Considering it gave him the perfect excuse to live on land with the woman he loved, Darkness thought it was more than fair.

Carman didn't owe them an explanation, but she gave one anyway. "He'll be just another denizen of Feyport visiting the carnival as far as the showmen are concerned. And if the water maiden tries to drown him, she'll not get very far considering his affinity for the ocean. Dain, since you seem to enjoy Declan's company so much, I think you can assist him with the rescue." Violence groaned even louder, throwing his head back in exaggerated dismay that had his mother chuckling. "And while you become the maiden's heroes, Dub and I shall take care of this mysterious magic."

"First," said Violence, "the seal can assist me, not the other way around. And second, what about showing the bastards the error of their ways?"

"Language. Please. Don't you worry. I've got something in mind."

This time Darkness couldn't help the frown that creeped onto his face.

Ten

BEFORE

"I can't imagine anyone, and I do mean anyone, Winnie, will pay a single copper coin to ride that thing." Enid stood arms crossed over her chest wearing the same expression she did when the horse stalls didn't get properly cleaned. It wasn't the stench of manure that had her grimacing however. It was the dilapidated remains of a children's attraction.

Several wooden horses were arranged on the spokes of a large oaken wheel. They were attached with springs that were meant to rock back and forth as the wheel was turned by a pair of the troupe's stronger hands. Unfortunately, half of the springs were rusted, and that was nothing compared to the state of the wood. The paint was chipped and peeling, the saddles split, several horses were missing a leg and one had only half a face. Were it meant to induce nightmares in either the riders or those hoping to profit from it, it was a startling success. Otherwise?

Bronwen had to agree with her sister. "I have no idea why he bought this thing." *Or where he found the money to buy it.*

"Girls! I see you've found my newest acquisition." Their father clapped as he bounded over to where they stood, frowning over the contraption.

Alfie Elwell was an average size man with a remarkably average face. But when he was excited, no one could deny he became something *more* than average. His energy could sway masses and his smile could conjure dreams.

A small group of showmen followed in his wake, but none of them approached where the sisters stood. This was one conversation they likely didn't want to be party to.

"But . . . why?" Enid scrunched up her nose. "You can't expect anyone to ride it."

"Ah, dear girl. A coat of paint and some oil in the springs and it will be a wonderful little gem. Something for the younger kiddies."

"But where did you get it?" she asked.

"*How* did you get it?" Bronwen added.

"Oh never mind that." He waved off the question.

"Da."

"Oh, all right. I ran into Old Sheffly last night. We were, well, it doesn't matter. Let's just say I didn't pay a single cent for the thing."

Albert Sheffly ran one of the smaller, more dingy competing troupes. Generally the circuits avoided one another, but every so often their paths would cross or the proprietors would be in the city at the same time. Bronwen suspected Sheffly was even more desperate than they were.

"You won it off him, you mean." Bronwen shook her head, disappointment in every line of her being.

"Does it matter?" The joy finally fell from his face. "The fact is it's ours now, and we need to spruce it up a bit before we can really add it to the show."

"It'll take more than sprucing," Enid countered. "It even smells bad. How does wood smell bad?"

"And yes, Da. It matters. What did you wager to begin with? What if you'd lost?" Bronwen pushed.

"I said it doesn't matter," he snapped. "Go on. Both of you. Ropes drop in an hour."

Enid's face was one of pure shock. Rarely if ever did their father raise his tone to them. "Da. We'll help you fix it up."

"I said go on, Enid. Oh and, Bronwen, make sure I see the take before you pay the troupe tonight."

"Come on." Bronwen grabbed her sister's hand and pulled her away from the worn-out attraction. She had no more desire to discuss the matter than her father did.

They pushed through the members of the troupe who'd gathered to take in the hulking wooden mess, CJ among them.

"Not exactly what I had in mind, Bronwen." He looked as confused as she felt.

"Can it, CJ. I'll figure it out." She sounded just as snappish as her father had.

"Figure what out?" Enid asked.

Bronwen waited until they were out of earshot. "Everything."

The crowd that night wasn't the best or the worst she'd seen. There were enough patrons to make the night profitable, but not enough to put them on the path to security. She sold plenty of candy floss and roasted peanuts, but the crowd for the most part stayed away from her higher-priced confections. She made a note to remember that not just for future nights on this stop, but for return visits as well.

It was thinning out and she was starting to pack up, her

back to the window, when a shadow fell over the opening. Her hands were full of dense toffee balls. "Just a moment and I will be right with you."

"Take one moment or two, Sweetling. Any longer and I shall be most offended."

It was him. The man from a few days prior.

She turned so abruptly one of the sticky toffee balls flew from her hand and directly into the cheek of the man standing at the window. It smacked his face then bounced and dribbled all down his chest.

"Oh. Oh, no. I am so sorry."

He was stunning. Stunning to the point it nearly took her breath from her lungs. Dark curls of hair framed a face that should not belong outside a dream. He had penetrating dark eyes, and in the flicker of the carnival lamps, she was unable to tell if they were actually jet or simply the richest shade of brown. His brows were thick and had an interesting arch that gave him a devilish appearance. It was only his ever so slightly crooked nose set above full lips and strong jaw, that made him look human. The one flaw that proved the rest real.

He lifted a hand and wiped at the tacky smudge on his cheek. "Do all patrons have syrupy messes thrust upon them?"

"Oh no. No, really. Let me grab—" She cast about for a cloth or rag to offer him. Seeing nothing immediately, she pulled the apron from her waist and ran down the back steps and around the front of the wagon to assist him.

Wiping furiously at first his face and then the stained and sticky shirt front, she had no idea what to say.

"Enough of that now." With one hand he stilled her frantic ministrations. The other, coated as it was in toffee syrup, he raised to his lips and tasted.

"Twice as tasty as suspected."

"Umm. thank you?"

"And there again is the countenance of a woman troubled."

"Troubled, sir? I just threw a pastry at you. Troubled doesn't quite cover it."

"Back to sir are we?"

"It *is* you then."

"I am me, yes."

"I mean to say, I spoke to you. Before. At the creek."

"Indeed, Mistress Sweetling, you did. And I see that you have thought enough of me to recognize me based on voice alone. I feel flattered."

"Well, yes, I recognized your voice." How could she not with its interesting cadence and even more interesting turns of phrase. "As for thinking of you, why wouldn't I, after you did your best to frighten me."

"Frightening you wasn't my intention."

"What then was your intention?" She continued to wipe ineffectually at his shirt front. "And for that matter, what are you doing here now?"

"I was intrigued by you. So full of life's burdens yet unwilling to share them. I thought to check up on you to see if your load had been lightened."

"I wish that I could say that it had."

"Pity."

She scrubbed at his shirt harder. "I don't wish your pity or any other's, sir."

He placed a hand on hers, stopping the cloth from moving further. "I've asked that you not call me that."

Flustered either by his touch or the conversation, a manic sort of giggle bubbled up. "You really expect me to call you Darkness?"

"As it is what I am named, yes. I expect I do." The last of the patrons trickled by as here and there the showmen packed up their stalls and tents.

She wasn't giggling any longer. Stepping back and crossing her arms, she said, "I don't enjoy being made a joke."

He cocked his head as he studied her, something birdlike in the gesture. A great bird of prey studying its next meal. "I expect not. But tell me, Sweetling, what do you suspect I do in jest?"

"Don't call me sweetling. My name is Bronwen. If that is too much, Miss Elwell will do."

He dipped his chin to her, a small smirk on his face. "As you like. Now, Bronwen, what is it you suspect I do to mock you?"

"Darkness? It's not a normal sort of name, is it? Do you find me so feeble of mind I'd believe you are more fey trickery than mortal man?" The lamp to the right of her winked, and she could hear glass tinkling as one of the games was packed up.

"Fey trickery? You offend me."

"Well, you offended me first by playing at being a monster meant to scare children into behaving themselves."

"And who says I am not such a monster?"

"Fine. Don't tell me your name."

"I much prefer the sweet side of you."

"And I prefer to know who I'm speaking with."

"What would it take to convince you I am not making jest?"

She scoffed and shook her head. "As you can see, the carnival is packing up for the night. Best if you find your way to the exit, *sir.*"

All around her the remaining lamps winked out and she was left in near total darkness. It was unsettling to say the least. Having him there before her one moment and seemingly gone the next.

She felt him just before she heard his voice at her ear. "Yes, *Sweetling,* I'll do just that."

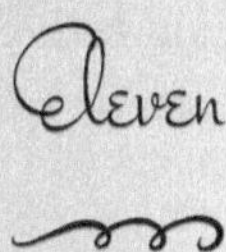

Eleven

" She's thinking really hard about that candy floss, isn't she?" The man's voice was more bemused than anything.

A sweet quiet voice replied. "Shhh, Tieg. Can't you see she's upset."

Tommy nudged her gently in the side and Bronwen snapped out of it.

She hadn't slept well the previous night. Each time she closed her eyes, her dreams were filled with bits and pieces of what she was now certain were old memories. With each flash she remembered a bit more, and now she was more certain than ever that she had known the man calling himself Darkness and maybe even known him well. Both youthful and vibrant. Perhaps he too was mixed up in this age-defying tribulation.

She still had no idea what he had to do with her life and why she couldn't piece it all together, but with each new memory, she became more and more convinced that CJ was hiding something from her. What was worse, she thought Enid might be playing a part in it as well.

That alone was enough to have her off kilter and distracted. Adding in the feeling that something very dark and very wrong was going on with Colger & Sons—girls caged in tanks, the sick feeling she had anytime she was near the carousel, the faces that should be old but were most definitely not. It was no wonder she couldn't focus on the tasks in front of her.

"My apologies." Bronwen looked out the wagon's window to find a pretty girl with dark shiny hair. In the flicker of the carnival lamps, it had an iridescent rainbow sheen to it, but that wasn't what surprised Bronwen the most. It was the small antlers that sprouted from the top of the woman's head which left her openly staring.

Feyport was living up to expectations it seemed.

She caught herself being uncharacteristically rude and blurted, "Oh! Here you go," while simultaneously flushing to her roots. She handed over two cones of soft pink candy floss. "Again, I apologize for the wait."

"Thank you," the girl said as she waved off the apology, obviously used to people gawking at her. "Hey. Do you mind if I ask you something?"

"Go ahead," Bronwen replied hesitantly.

"I'm just wondering what attractions you suggest. This is our first time at the carnival and when I asked the ticket taker, he was adamant we try the carousel but told us to wait til close to closing, I assume that means it's pretty popular. So we wanted to do some other things first."

Dread rose up in Bronwen, and without thinking, she blurted, "No. Stay away from the carousel."

The girl flinched back. The man with her grabbed her elbow in comfort, jaw set and brow furrowed in Bronwen's direction.

Bronwen shut her eyes and gave her head a little shake before taking a deep breath. She tried to smile at the pair but knew it was a poor attempt. "I . . . sorry. I just think you should stay off the carousel tonight. It's been malfunctioning. You wouldn't enjoy the ride."

The girl with the antlers nodded, clearly unconvinced by the lie.

"If you're looking for something jaw dropping, take in the show in the big top. It's fantastic. You can also try the mirror maze and the curiosities tent. They're both a lot of fun."

The pair were joined by two more women. They had to be sisters by the look of it. Both had thick red hair, one the color of copper and the other a deeper auburn.

"I'm up for the mirror maze. What do ya say, Fia?"

"Sounds good," the girl with the antlers said.

"And what about that wagon in the back? The one painted in all the beautiful shades of blue?" It was the girl with the copper hair. "Reminds me of water."

"You would notice a wagon that looks like the water, wouldn't you, Aylee?" the auburn-haired woman teased.

Bronwen wasn't sure what to say. She'd already acted a little crazed when she told them to stay away from the carousel. "Oh, that attraction is empty. Nothing in there but storage now. You'll want to stick to the things in the front and center of the site."

The words felt stiff, and she could tell they didn't fully believe her. The man raised his cone of candy floss and dipped his head in thanks, then began to lead the others away.

"Wait," Bronwen called, and all four of the group turned and looked at her. She ran down the steps and waved her hand to pull them safely out of the aisle. Thoughts of CJ and his newfound willingness to do unscrupulous things wouldn't allow her to let them wander off without some sort of warning.

"It might be best to leave the show before it gets too late." She chewed at her lower lip, shooting glances back and forth up the alleyway around her wagon. She looked pointedly at the girl with the antlers. "And stay together, yeah."

"Yeah, all right," the girl responded. "Thanks."

When she returned to the wagon, Tommy gave her a relieved smile.

"I'm sure CJ will have a fit if he hears I'm steering people away from it, but. . ." She shrugged.

Tommy patted her lightly on the shoulder.

"I know, you don't like it either."

She remembered she had been going to get him the slate to tell her why exactly when they'd been interrupted days earlier. With the show in full swing, she didn't think now was the time to have him scribbling it out, but she made a mental note to ask him the following day.

The calliope music was going full tilt, and the chatter of the crowd was growing with each bag of candied almonds and every glob of taffy she sold. The bonbons were once again a hit, and she'd sold all but one of them. Without thinking, she pulled it from the case and wrapped it in a square of waxed paper. She set it to the side and continued the business of providing sugar-coated dreams to the patrons from Feyport.

Eventually, the crowd thinned enough for Tommy to leave her on her own, and she felt a wave of guilt for being happy he was gone. She always enjoyed having him around, but with her tired feet and distracted mind, she was ready to be alone for a spell.

Gradually, the crowd thinned to a trickle. When it was down to the last patrons, mostly young men who'd partaken of the attractions as well as some libations, she closed the wagon window and pulled the coins from the till. When she exited the back, something told her to leave the small waxed morsel on the top step. With that done, she left to go find CJ and give him his portion of her earnings.

She found him as she always did, surveying the site in slow

measured steps. He never liked to sit still, always walking the show from rope drop to take down. Always moving. Always watching.

At his age, he wasn't as quick as he'd once been, but he still did it every night.

She saw him near the carousel, a deep scowl on his face.

She was ready to turn and go the other direction, determined to stay as far from the thing as possible, but he caught sight of her. He raised a hand and waved her over.

It would do no good to let him see how uncomfortable she was. It would only irritate him and she'd still need to give him his share, so she gritted her teeth and met him where he stood. Unfortunately, where he stood happened to be right next to a wooden goblin. The thing was on all fours to allow for the ride's saddle. It wore a grimace of either pain or lunacy or maybe both. Its head turned sideways as if glaring at anyone it passed on its endless looping turns.

CJ didn't say anything as he held out his hand and she dropped a bag of coins into it.

The bruising on his face had faded, but he had a diminished look about him. Always thin, he now looked almost skeletal.

She shivered.

He bounced the coin bag and she knew he was weighing it as he did every night. "You did well this evening, it seems."

"The crowd was decent."

"It was. I was hoping tonight would be an invigorating night. But it didn't quite live up to my expectations." He continued to scowl at the carousel. "It's interesting." He paused, expecting her to ask what he meant.

She didn't.

He turned his scowl on her then. "Do you know, this is the first night the carousel hasn't had a line a dozen deep all evening?"

"No," she answered. "How would I know that when I spend all my time on the far side of the show, selling confections?"

He twisted his lips to the side and made a clucking sort of sound. "Hmm. Well, let's hope tomorrow proves a better showing. If not, there's always. . ." He seemed distracted, thinking about something only he knew.

"Always what?'

"Nothing." He snapped his attention back to her. "I've been thinking about Neeve."

"Neeve?"

"Our new addition. The water maiden."

Bronwen didn't want to know how he'd gotten her name. She assumed the woman wouldn't have shared it willingly. Perhaps whoever he'd acquired her from had told him. That's what she hoped at least.

"I've been thinking. You were right. I can't simply put her on display. She could just be any woman for all *they* know." *They.* The patrons. There was such loathing in the one word, but who were they without their audience? "It's not a big enough draw for the risks."

"CJ, just let her go. There's no payoff large enough to justify keeping her against her will."

He looked at her like he was seeing her for the first time and he was duly unimpressed. "All these years and you still don't understand what it takes to be a success."

"I don't want success."

"You do Bronwen. Everyone does, in one form or another. You can't tell me otherwise."

"Not like this."

"Like this is the only way there is."

The goblin glared at her from its tormented spot on the carousel. She couldn't stay there any longer. Not near the horrid ride. Not near the man she thought she knew but clearly didn't. And maybe not in the place she called home for much longer.

If she could ensure the girl in the tank was set free, she might just slip away one night.

The sound of drunken laughter snagged her attention. Up ahead, a man stumbled along, bumping into one of the fairy wing stalls. She was making her way over to him, when she saw Kerb. The old showman smiled at her.

Waving her off, he called, "I'll help this gent find the exit. No need to bother you, Bron."

"All right, Kerb. Good night."

He was talking calmly to the intoxicated patron and leading him off toward the exit when he called back, "You too, Bron. You too."

The next morning Bronwen discovered two things.

A smooth ochre-colored stone resting on the back step of the confectionary wagon in place of the sweet she had left there and Kerb looking not a day over twenty-five.

"Not this again." Enid sighed. "Really, Winnie, it's getting to be a bit of a bore."

They were standing outside the big top. After seeing Kerb turn back the clock by decades, Bronwen knew something terrible really was going on in the carnival. Something she had obviously been a party to. She'd made up her mind to leave as soon as she helped Darkness free the water maiden but couldn't fathom the idea of leaving without telling Enid first. Maybe she could even convince her sister to come with her.

Bronwen didn't know how to reply. She'd just told her sister she was thinking of leaving the troupe, and instead of tears and outrage, she was met with little more than indifference.

Surely she hadn't heard correctly. "A bore?"

"Yes. A bore. Honestly. We do this every time."

Bronwen's stomach lurched. There it was again. *Every time.* What had they done and how many times?

Enid must have seen how distraught she was. She softened.

"You're still feeling confused. I understand, but you can't just leave. What would I do without you?"

"You can come with me."

"I could, but I won't, Winnie. This is my home. Our home."

"What about the city? You've always wanted to live in the city, Enid."

"The city? That was ages ago, Winnie. Honestly." She looked at Bronwen, and the pitch of her voice changed. It was like she was explaining things to a small child or an addled person. But in a way, Bronwen supposed she was. "We have everything we need here. You just need to let CJ handle things. He always does. He takes care of us, remember."

"I wish you would stop telling me what I need to do. And no, I don't remember." Bronwen rarely raised her voice to Enid, but she was so frustrated. So tired. So confused. So lonely. And the one person she felt she should be able to rely on to help her through it was only making it worse.

"Fine," Enid snapped back. "Should I tell you what you've forgotten?"

"Yes," Bronwen begged. "Please."

"What would you like to know then?"

"You said every time. Have we done this before? Gone from old to young?"

Enid raised her brows and smirked. "Yes."

Bronwen wasn't sure she really wanted to know. Her voice was small when she asked, "How many?"

"How many what?"

"Times. How many times have we done this? Turned back the clock?"

"Four."

Bronwen sat down hard. Four times. How could it be *four times*? That was centuries worth of time. It couldn't possibly be.

"How?'

"That isn't for me to share."

"Then who?" Bronwen demanded.

"It doesn't matter," Enid said nonchalantly.

"Is it CJ? Does he do this?"

"Not exactly, but he allows it."

"Why?"

"Because we can, Winnie."

"Everyone?"

"No. Not everyone. Only a handful of us."

"But the others allow it?"

"Well, they don't really know, do they?" Again she said it like Bronwen was daft for suggesting such a thing.

But that couldn't be? There was bound to be some sort of overlap, wasn't there? They had to see certain members of the troupe getting younger? Kerb for instance. But then she thought about how stretched thin they'd been, taking on temporary help here and there but really working with just a small core of the troupe.

"The rest come and go as they've always done," Enid explained. "None the wiser."

Bronwen thought immediately of Tommy. He seemed like such a good person. She hoped he had no idea what was going on around him. She hoped he'd leave the troupe soon before he figured it out.

"And you remember it all?'

"All of what?"

"All of everything. All those years."

"Of course I do. We all do. Well, aside from you. It seems worse this time for you though. You usually start to remember things by a week or two after."

"Why? Why can't I remember, Enid?" Desperation. *This* is what desperation sounds like, she thought.

"I can't say." Enid wouldn't look at her when she answered.

"Can't or won't?"

"Does it matter?"

"Yes, Enid, to me it does."

Enid pushed her sweaty hair from her face. "Look, Winnie. I need to clean up and get ready for the show."

"But I don't . . . I wouldn't . . . Enid? Whatever this is, however we do this, have I wanted this, Enid?"

Her desperation was met by Enid's pity.

"Like I said, I need to get ready for the show."

Thirteen

Days went by as if Bronwen'd never met the strange man. She made her treats and attempted to keep the bulk of the proceeds from her father's hands. It made her feel ill to have to go to such lengths, particularly after he'd expressly told her to give him the coins. Several of the troupe brought her their collections, but most handed them over to him. He was the proprietor after all.

For his part, her father had returned to a somewhat jovial state. He never spoke of the exchange with her, nor did he ask her about the money he must have known she was withholding. In fact, he pretended everything was fine.

He worked tirelessly on the restoration of the wooden horses, making small improvements that kept the thing from being a complete atrocity. He painted each equine mount a different pastel shade, oiled the springs, and applied fresh ropes and cloth to complete the saddles and stirrups. He even dug out an old automated grind organ that the showman running the ride could play while the children went round and round.

It would still be days before the ride would debut at the carnival, but for now, it was being packed up, just like the rest of the show.

It was time to move out. Bronwen wasn't sure whether she was happy about the fact or not. While it was always refreshing to tear down and start again in a new town or village, she was left feeling unsettled.

She hadn't expected her unusual visitor to show up again, not after how things had gone the last time she saw him. Still, she was a tad disappointed each night he stayed away.

Climbing into the wagon she was sharing with Enid and several of the other performers, CJ included, she thought she caught a flicker of movement in the trees. She stopped midway up the ladder of stars, searching the vegetation.

"By all means, do take your time, Winnie." Enid stood on the ground just behind her, impatiently tapping her foot.

"Sorry." Bronwen hauled herself the remainder of the way up and settled on one of the benches in the back of the conveyance. Enid sat beside her, CJ across. Within minutes, the horses began to pull and the wagon joined the train making their way from the site.

"You haven't been yourself in days. Let's have it then," Enid said.

Bronwen looked to the others sitting around them. "I don't know what you're talking about." Three of the troupe had fallen asleep almost as soon as the wagon began moving, but CJ was wide awake, whittling a piece of wood into the form of a mermaid.

"Yes, you do. Something has you distracted."

Bronwen dropped her voice. "I'd rather not discuss it now, Enid."

"Still thinking about finding yourself a *man*," her sister teased.

"Enid." Her eyes jumped to the other troupe members filling the wagon.

"Oh, come on. They're all asleep, and even if they weren't, it's not like they wouldn't understand. We all need a distraction every now and then."

"What're you talking about?" CJ asked, not looking up from the full bosom he was forming with his knife.

"Nothing," Bronwen said.

"Winnie thinks the troupe is filled with too many boys and not enough men," Enid supplied.

"Enid, that's enough." Brownen loved her sister, but sometimes Enid took things a little too far. She would think a joke at someone else's expense could be the most hilarious thing, not realizing until it was too late the damage she had done.

CJ finally looked up from his bit of willow. "Is that true?"

"We aren't talking about this," Bronwen said.

"Well, saints and sinners, Bronwen, if I'd of known you needed a little company, I'd be more than happy to—"

"Do not finish that sentence, CJ," Bronwen seethed.

"Didn't you hear me say she's looking for a man, CJ?" Enid taunted. "*Not* a boy."

CJ flushed a bright tomato from the tips of his ears down his neck.

"I think I'll walk for a bit." Bronwen rose to exit the back of the wagon.

"Oh, for the love of the stars, Winnie. Sit down. I'll behave."

Against her better judgment, Bronwen did as her sister said.

"I'm only teasing you both. You can't go and find a man anyhow. What would I do without you?"

"Better yet," CJ interjected, his color returning to normal. "What would the troupe do without you?"

"It's not her job to worry about the troupe, CJ. We've talked about it."

"You've talked about it? The two of you?" Bronwen asked.

"Of course we have." Enid gave her sister a withering look. "CJ thinks you need to take over."

"You what?" Bronwen was more than a little shocked by the revelation. She didn't mind helping out, but her father was the proprietor. She wouldn't want to take that from him, and she didn't think anyone in the troupe wanted it either.

"Come on, Enid. I didn't say that exactly," CJ said.

"Well then, what did you say?" Bronwen prompted him.

He sighed and ran a hand over his face. "I don't want to be in the middle of this."

"Ha!" barked Enid. "That's a laugh. That is exactly what you want. You told me yourself: you think Winnie needs to find some amazing attraction to keep the carnival going. How is that Winnie's job?"

"It's not. But if she doesn't do it, who will?" CJ demanded.

"Why don't you do it, if you know so much," Enid said.

"You think I wouldn't. I've given the old man more than a dozen suggestions, and he just keeps putting me off. I swear sometimes I think he wants the place to fail."

"He's got the new thing he's been working on," Bronwen said. Unfortunately she didn't sound overly convincing. "That's something at least."

"That thing is a travesty and you know it, Winnie."

"It's not that bad."

"I'm going to have to side with Enid on this one," CJ said. "Those springs? It barely moves. The least he could do is get a fully automated carousel."

"With what money?" Bronwen asked. Talking to Enid

about this was one thing, but involving CJ to this level left her feeling guilty. But CJ had a point. The little wooden ride was about as likely to save them as Enid was.

"That's what I'm saying. We need a real showstopper."

"Yes. You've said that before. Problem is, I have no idea where to get this showstopper."

"Listen." He leaned forward conspiratorially, looking at the others who were still asleep. "I've got this buddy, from back home. He was at the show last week, and he told me he knew a guy who had some family in the city, and they aren't all *exactly* aboveboard."

"We are not doing anything illegally," Bronwen said with as much steel as she could muster. "I mean it, CJ."

He waved her off. "Of course not. That isn't what I'm saying. It's just that he mentioned they have all sorts of connections. If we can get put in contact with someone, we can offer to pay them. Real honest work. Nothing illegal. We just need to find them."

"What sort of people are we talking about?" Enid asked.

He held up the wooden trinket. "A mermaid."

Bronwen sighed. "Oh, for heaven's sake, CJ."

"No, Bronwen, really. He said he's seen her himself."

"And this mermaid wants to 'work' in a carnival?" She held her hand to her forehead, embarrassed she'd let this conversation go on for as long as it had.

"Sure. Why not?"

"Well, for one, they live in the sea. I don't think anyone who lives in the sea is signing up to be in a tank for folks from the heartlands to gawk at."

"You don't know that. But all right. He says the family has other fey on their payroll. A guy with horns and even a banshee."

Enid snorted. "No wonder Da didn't want to listen to you." Bronwen couldn't disagree.

"Look, all I'm saying is there are big things out there whether you want to believe it or not. We just need to find one."

"Sure, CJ. We'll keep our eyes open."

With that, Bronwen tilted her head back, closed her eyes, and feigned falling asleep.

It was the next week when she saw the handsome dark-haired man again. He didn't speak to her or approach her in any way.

She looked up one afternoon while making pralines and saw him watching her from the edge of the forest. She'd put a hand up to block the sun from her eyes, and when she looked again, he was gone. That night on the steps leading from the back of the confection wagon, she found a smoothly polished riverstone. It was a deep grey speckled with obsidian flecks.

The following day, she thought she saw him standing under the eaves of the mercantile when she'd gone to town to pick up a crate of eggs. Enid had hurried her along, so she wasn't able to see if it had been him for certain, but that night after closing up the wagon, another stone greeted her. This one was a smooth flawless caramel color. It was slightly larger than one of the eggs she'd purchased and cool to the touch.

The pattern continued for almost two weeks: her catching a glimpse of him but never getting the chance to talk or berate him for his odd behavior. After closing finding a small stone waiting for her on the steps. They had picked up the carnival and moved it twice, and still he appeared and disappeared, and then the stone.

She worried the behavior should frighten her, but it didn't.

She wondered if she should tell someone what was happening, but she wouldn't.

She hoped he would eventually seek her out to explain, and eventually, he did.

When her collection of rocks had grown to a small heap, and she was beginning to wonder if she could just throw them all back into the next stream they crossed, she exited the wagon one night and found the man, not a stone, sitting on the steps.

He was tossing something in the air and catching it repeatedly.

"Hello?" The simple greeting came out as a question. She was more than a little pleased to see him, if only to ask why he'd been following her. It was perilous and foolish and a thousand other un-Bronwen–like things to be, but something about him enthralled her. That too should have worried her.

He didn't turn to her as he answered. "Sweetling." He caught what he'd been tossing and placed it in his pocket.

"What are you doing here?"

"In the neighborhood and thought I'd come by for a treat."

"I see. Unfortunately, the wagon is all closed up for the night," she said.

"And no accommodation can be made?"

She bit back her smile. "Give me a moment."

Bronwen went back inside and returned with a small parcel. It was a soft pale cloth tied with a bit of red twine. She held it out to him.

"What would you ask as payment?"

She continued to hold it out to him. "No payment."

"I'm afraid I can't allow that." He reached into his pocket and held out his hand.

In his palm was a stone no bigger than a quail's egg. It was almost perfectly round, shiny and smooth. And the darkest onyx black she'd ever seen. Surely this stone hadn't come from any riverbed or creek in these parts.

"I . . . that isn't necessary. It looks much too valuable."

"It is only a stone." He cocked his head and smiled. "I insist."

She delicately plucked the dark rock from his hand, and he took the small parcel from hers. She studied the small rock. "It's lovely. Thank you."

He inclined his head and unwrapped the packet she'd given him. Inside lay a smooth pink confection, not much larger than the stone he'd traded for it. The shell of the goodie was solid but delicate, with a small flower embellishment in the center.

"It's a cherry and cream bonbon. It's one of my signature creations."

He bit into it, and his eyes widened with just the barest trace of surprise. The center was light and airy and creamy and wonderful. Bronwen beamed as he chewed and swallowed the first bite and immediately ate the second half.

He didn't speak but licked the sugary traces off his fingers. Bronwen was surprised to admit to herself she was entranced watching him eat the small delicacy.

When she could stand his silence no longer, she prodded. "Well?"

"It was divine."

She sensed he was holding something back. "But?"

"I don't wish to offend."

Her smile fell. She had been sure he'd enjoyed it, but apparently she'd been wrong. It shouldn't matter one way or the other, but sadly it did. She was still irked that he wouldn't tell her who he really was, but she had so wanted him to like it.

"You didn't like it?"

"Quite the contrary. Delectable, in fact. Sugary sweet. Like you but unlike you. No sharpness to balance it out."

"I'm not sharp."

He raised a single eyebrow. "No?"

"Well, perhaps a smidge. On my off days."

"A smidge," he agreed.

"Hmm." She thought on it. "You might be right."

"I am seldom wrong."

She snorted and shook her head. "A bit of citrus maybe. Lemon? No, that'd be too bitter and orange would clash." She shrugged. It would niggle at her until she thought of the right combination, but often these things took her some time to tease out correctly. She elected to change the subject. "So, *Darkness*, you've been following us. Why?"

"Ah. There. See? Sharp. Must be an off day."

"Mmm-hmm." She sat on the step, and he sat down next to her.

"Is it a problem to find the carnival intriguing?" he asked.

"Not a problem to be intrigued for a night or two. It's been weeks and you've moved right along with us. That isn't typical."

"I've never been accused of being typical."

"Don't you have a home? Somewhere comfy and cozy to spend your nights? A job? People to tend to?" she asked.

"My home is everywhere. Sometimes it's cozy but not often. Sometimes it's *comfy*"—the way he said the word made her grin—"but not regularly. My job is to do as I am bid, and when I am called, I will answer. For now the people I tend to do not need me."

"You never speak plainly, do you?"

"I've never felt plainlyness suited me."

"You are so odd." She smiled as she said it, and if it offended him, he didn't show it.

"It is not in my nature to be other than I am. I wish at times to change my nature, but not so often as to do it."

"And what is in your nature then?"

"I've told you before. As my name implies, so too is my nature."

"What does that even mean?" The words were strained, but she felt her laughter bubbling up.

"Exactly what you think it does." He didn't sound taunting or teasing, just matter-of-fact as if it should all be evident.

She sighed.

It had been a lovely night and Bronwen didn't wish to ruin it just yet, so she didn't argue or ask him to elaborate.

The air was cool and the tree boughs were singing their sweet songs and the humid breeze danced through them. People milled about packing up their stalls or meeting for a bite or a pint before they all turned in for the night. A handful of fireflies bounced along in the darkness.

They sat in companionable silence until she asked, "So what do the stones mean?'

"Must they mean something?"

"I just figured, since you were leaving me one each night, there must be a meaning to it." She stopped, embarrassed. "They are for me, aren't they?"

"Indeed they are."

She blew out a breath of relief.

He smiled again. "They are fascinating, are they not? So strong and seemingly indestructible but worn smooth with time and the currents. I find them beautiful and thought you might as well."

"But why leave me anything at all? Or do you leave trinkets and baubles for all the women you follow in secret?"

He chuckled. "You are my first."

He really was the most striking man she'd ever seen. When he laughed she felt it right in the center of her chest.

"Oh, hello, hello," a light musical voice chirped. Bronwen cringed. Why did Enid have to show up just when Bronwen least wanted her there? "Oh, Winnie. Who might this be?"

She froze. She couldn't possibly introduce the man as Darkness. Enid would go crazy with it and offend him for sure.

"This is my sister Enid. Enid, this is. . ." She cast around for a way to make the introduction without being rude or sounding like a fool.

"Just a friend," he answered for her as he stood. "One who must be on his way."

"Oh, please don't leave on my account." Enid, still in full makeup and her most daring performance outfit, was a vision for any man to behold and she knew it. Short blonde hair pulled back with sequined combs and sparkles adorning every inch of her trunk, she left her legs and arms bare. In any other setting, it might be thought of as scandalous. "Winnie and I were just chatting about the benefits of finding a good handsome man. And you are definitely handsome. I'm guessing you're also good." She winked at her sister.

Bronwen wanted nothing more than to crawl into a ball and hide under the stairs.

"I've not been accused of being good in quite a long while." His eyes held a devilish gleam. He dipped his head to Bronwen. "Have a good evening, ladies."

He was several paces away when he stopped and turned back. "Oh, and Bronwen?"

"Yes?"

"Lime perhaps?"

Only two small words, but Bronwen knew immediately what he meant. And she knew he was right. Lime would be the perfect tart balance to the sweetness of the cherry. She could already imagine the taste coating her tongue.

"What the stars does that mean?" Enid asked as she

dropped down on the step Darkness had just vacated. "Better yet, *who* the stars was that?"

"Just a friend."

"Right. And I am just a girl. Winnie, that man was the most delicious thing I've seen near this wagon in ages, and you know how much I adore your custard tartlets."

Bronwen snorted as she tried to contain her laughter. Enid's ridiculousness was one of the things she adored most about her sister. No matter the occasion, she could always make her laugh. Or cringe. There was seldom anything in between.

"If you don't start spilling soon, I'll be forced to take drastic measures."

"How drastic?"

"Telling CJ you fancy him drastic." Enid laughed. "You know he'll believe me."

"You wouldn't dare." Bronwen pushed her sister's shoulder. "You know I only think of him as a brother, if that. It'd be cruel."

"True. But I'm not above a little cruelty. Plus, it'd get him away from me. Honestly, you'd think he'd pick one or the other of us instead of just hoping either of us would take him."

Bronwen looked at her sister askance. "He's been flirty with you his whole life. Not me. If you aren't interested, you should tell him so."

"He should have figured it out by now. Besides, we aren't talking about me right now. I want to know who that devilishly handsome man is and what you two were doing together." Her eyes went wide. "Is he *The Man*? The one who is going to elevate himself above all the boys? Oh, Winnie. Tell me he is."

"It's hard to elevate oneself when I still don't know his name."

"Still? What does that mean? How long have you been talking to him?"

"It's only been a few times. Do you remember me mentioning someone playing a trick on me?"

"The witch's son?! Winnie. That's him? Darkness?"

Bronwen chewed at her lower lip as she nodded.

"Saints and sinners. Was he bothering you again? We should do something. Have Da put up tighter security."

"I don't really think that's necessary."

"But that was ages ago. In that other little town. Did he follow you here?"

Enid's reaction wasn't at all what Bronwen had expected, and it made her feel like maybe she should be more concerned. She'd been a bit frightened that first day by the creek, and then more annoyed than anything. Tonight, however, she hadn't been concerned by him at all. True, she was irritated he wouldn't tell her his real identity, but it felt more like a ridiculous game between friends than a menacing ploy of some sort. For all his strangeness, she felt comfortable with him.

"It's nothing like that, Enid. He's rather kind actually."

"Winnie. He calls himself Darkness and has tracked you down. That is not normal behavior." She grasped her sister's hands. "Wait. How many times have you two spoken?"

"Just a few, but. . ."

But he's been watching me every day and leaving me stones each night. It did sound a little off.

"But?"

"But it's nothing. He just wanted a confection and got here a little late. It isn't anything to worry about," Bronwen said. "Besides, we have bigger concerns than who I'm chatting with. Nobody brought me their coins tonight. That means they've all given them to Da. I just hope he's putting them away and not throwing them away."

"Nothing you can do about it now even if he is." Enid

pulled Bronwen up with her as she stood. "You're certain I don't need to be concerned about this man bothering you?"

Bronwen wasn't certain at all, but she felt weirdly protective of him all the same.

"I'm certain. Come on. Let's grab a bite while it's still warm. Then I'm heading to bed. I'm knackered."

Fourteen

BEFORE

It wasn't often that Bronwen was able to leave her wagon and wander the carnival while it was in full swing, but when word the next night spread about her amazing new cherry-lime bonbons and the crowd descended early, she sold out of goodies well before the close of the show. Every lolly, each paper cone of candy floss, all the cookies and tartlets, every single sugar mouse and each and every jelly drop, plus all of her sacks of caramel popping corn were gone right along with the bonbons. Only a handful of hard candies remained—certainly not enough to keep the wagon open. Well, a handful of hard candies and one cherry-lime bonbon. Rather than do the responsible thing and whip up extras, she shuttered the serving window, pocketed her earnings, wrapped the bonbon in waxed paper, and headed for the big top.

It had been ages since she'd watched Enid in a full performance. She often caught glimpses of her practice routines and training with the other death-defying performers, but she was always too busy herself to take in the full spectacle.

Entering the tent and grabbing a seat near the performers' entrance was easy. It was a space not offered to the general patrons, which was all for the better as the ropes and swings were partially obstructed from view there. Bronwen didn't mind though. She could see enough to have her heart in her throat for her sister.

Enid was fearless. Blessed with a natural grace and uncanny balance, she made the tricks look as natural as walking or breathing. Loud gasps and awws filled the tent as trick after trick went off without a hitch. First Enid was walking the rope, a small umbrella in one hand and the other stretched out before her. Then she was swinging suspended at the knees and releasing just in time to be caught by the strong and able hands of Clive, her partner in most performances.

Despite Clive being a good ten years older than Enid, for a time Bronwen had fancied Enid and Clive a secret couple. That was before Clive surprised them all by introducing his wife one lazy afternoon. Maggie, a quiet woman of about his own age, had come to the carnival one night, and they'd fallen madly in love when she offered him a single daffodil after his show. She left her job in the city as a florist to join them on the circuit and had been selling crowns woven through with everything from daisies to marigolds to great bunches of hyacinth ever since.

Maggie snuck in after Bronwen and dropped down on the bench beside her. She had the crowns lining her left arm. Maggie didn't have a set stall, preferring rather to wander the grounds selling her creations on the move.

"I never get tired of watching him."

Bronwen reached a hand around and gave the other women a squeeze from the side. "He's magnificent. There aren't many others I'd trust to catch her every time." They watched in silence for a few more minutes. When the finale ended and the crowd was on their feet roaring, they both stood and clapped along.

"Well, I'm off," Maggie said. "Still got a dozen crowns left. I'm hoping to unload them all before the end of the night."

"I'm sure they'll be gone in minutes," Bronwen said.

"Oh. I almost forgot. I was on my way in and saw someone who looked distinctly displeased that you weren't at your wagon."

"Oh? Who was it?"

"Not sure. Tall fellow." Maggie stretched her hand up well above her head. "Dark hair. Do you know him?"

"Thanks, Mags. I have an idea."

Maggie left to sell her remaining crowns, and Brownen followed shortly after. With any luck, she'd find Darkness before anyone else did.

He wasn't by the pink and white wagon when she got there, and she assumed she'd missed him for the night. She hadn't glimpsed him all day, and no stone was waiting on her steps.

It was a little disappointing if she admitted it to herself. They were due to pack up the next day, and she wasn't sure he'd follow them again. Maybe Enid really had scared him off.

Rather than wallow in her disappointment, she trotted up the steps, grabbed the treat she'd wrapped in waxed paper, and headed for her personal wagon. She could at least enjoy the treat herself before going to bed later in the evening.

She was opening the door to the space she shared with Enid when one of the shadows pulled from the side of the wagon and stepped toward her.

The yelp that escaped her was not one of her finer moments.

"Sweetling. My apologies for the startle."

"Saints and sinners. Maybe you're a witch's son after all."

"Not *a*, Sweetling. *The*. *The* Witch."

"We're still playing this game, are we?"

"Not a game. You still doubt me." It wasn't a question.

"I suppose I do."

"What have you in your hand?"

Startled and a touch exasperated by the change in topic, she chuckled and shook her head. "It's for you actually. I meant to give it to you at the confectionery, but I left early to watch part of the show."

"Your sister does have an immense talent."

"Oh? Did you see her perform?"

"I did. A few nights ago." He placed his hands behind his back and rocked back slightly on his heels. "I've a wager to propose."

"I'm afraid you've got the wrong Elwell. It's my da you'll be looking for if you're a gambling man." The words were out before she meant to speak them, and she regretted them immediately. She didn't know this man well enough to spill those sorts of family secrets.

He cocked an eyebrow. "Interesting. A deal then, not a wager. We may both win in the end."

As it had been with this man several times already, her curiosity was raised. "All right. What is your proposal?"

"Let me convince you I am who I claim, and in return you will give me that morsel in your hand."

"But I was already going to give it to you."

He didn't argue with her. "May I?"

"But why would you want to? Even if you are the Darkness of stories, why does it matter to you that I believe such a thing?"

"I've asked myself the same question a dozen plus a dozen times. I do not have an answer. It only matters to me that you do."

She looked at him a moment. "You don't seem menacing when you say things like that."

"I only menace when need be."

She snorted a laugh. "And what if you still don't convince me?"

"Your doubts don't wound as you may suspect. I know what I know. And soon you shall too."

Shaking her head, she smiled and said, "All right then. Convince me."

The sounds of laughter and merriment drifted from the carnival proper. Lights twinkled on the grounds and the stars twinkled from the skies above. A whisper of a breeze danced over the exposed skin of her neck and arms.

The most handsome man she had ever seen stood before her framed by all of this—a smirk on his face. She couldn't help but smile back.

She blinked and he was gone—nothing before her but the darkest of night's shadows.

She looked around dumbfounded.

He hadn't moved, she was certain of it. Even if she hadn't seen him move with her eyes, she would have heard the crunch of the gravel under his boots.

"Darkness?"

"Yes, Sweetling?"

She jumped. His voice was right next to her ear. Not unlike it had been all those nights before. She could feel him there. Hear him there. She could even smell him—just the faintest mix of clove and cedar and woodsmoke.

But she could not *see* him.

"Where are you?"

"Right where you know me to be."

"How?"

"You might as well ask me how I make my heart beat or my lungs draw breath. It simply is."

He grabbed her hand, and when she looked down she

could see the shadow of his hand grabbing hers. "Now, let us continue."

"Continue?"

"I'm to convince you, am I not?"

"Yes?"

"Then we continue." And as she looked at where she knew their hands to be clasped, the shadow grew, traveling up the length of her arm to her elbow and then shoulder. She held her breath as it crept farther, and she could see it travel over her chest.

"Breathe, Sweetling." His words were soft but commanding.

She did, and as she exhaled, she sensed the shadow envelope her wholly. The moment she was inside the gloom she could see Darkness as clearly as if it were noon on a cloudless day. The area surrounding them had grown murky and smudged. It wasn't just the lights though. Even the carnival sounds were dampened. Gone too was the smell of manure and popping corn.

"What's happened?"

"Nothing tragic, I assure you. It's no more than a trick of the dark. Bending the gloom and shadows to do as I beg. You are still you and the world is still there."

"It's quite extraordinary."

"For me it's actually most ordinary." He released her hand and dropped the shadow and everything was as it had been minutes before. The cacophony of her life returned with a rush.

"So tell me, Sweetling, does doubt still weigh on you?"

"I don't see how it could. I don't actually know what to say."

"I suggest you say you're going to give me that bonbon." His smile was wicked and wild, and if she hadn't just stepped

into the night itself, she would have found it the most aston-
ishing thing she had ever seen.

Looking back, Bronwen knew that was the night she
started falling in love for the first and only time in her life.

❦

CJ and Enid found her the next morning.

"I knew you could do it," CJ said.

She'd just finished her breakfast and was heading
back to secure her wagon before the horses were attached and
they got on their way again.

"I'm sorry. Do what?" Bronwen asked him.

"Save the show."

"I have no idea what you're talking about."

"Right." He laughed. "You trying to make it a surprise or
something? Are you in on this too, Enid?"

"I am afraid I have not a single clue what you are on
about." Enid rolled her neck on her shoulders, clearly uninter-
ested in the conversation.

"Make what a surprise?" Bronwen asked.

"Fine. I'll play along." He smiled and wrapped a hand
around her shoulder as they walked toward the waiting
wagons. "Dearest Bronwen. Please tell me all about the new
act."

"CJ. I don't know what you are talking about. I haven't
found a new act." She unceremoniously removed his hand
from her shoulder and dropped it to his side.

He continued on as if she hadn't spoken. "I just don't
know how it works. I've been trying to pull it apart all night. Is
it a trick of the lighting or a thin fabric veil of some sort? I'd
love to think it was actually magic, but it's not like any I've
heard about before and you didn't believe me about the fey, so
it's got to be an illusion. At any rate, it's sure to draw crowds

from miles round. We can name him something catchy if he doesn't have a performance name yet. Master of Midnight or something. Put Enid in a little black costume and she could be his assistant."

"I'm no one's *assistant*, thanks."

Bronwen stopped walking, an unsettled feeling building in her stomach. "CJ. Tell me what you're talking about."

"What? You want to be the assistant? I suppose if you did up your hair. . ."

"CJ, stop." Bronwen held up a hand. "What are you talking about?"

"Fine. I'm *talking* about the new act you were working with last night by your wagon. The tall bloke with the dark hair. I was worried at first. I'd not seen him around before. Thought you might need a bit of rescuing. Some of the lads in these little hovels can get a bit lonely and all. Anyway. I was coming over to shoo him off, and then I thought it was a trick of the light when I couldn't see him anymore, but then you disappeared too, only to pop right back a moment later. It's as fine a trick as I've ever seen."

Oh no. No, no, no. She had to cut off this line of talk quickly. CJ could run his mouth like nobody else when he had a mind to. The last thing she needed was for the whole troupe —her father included—thinking she had scouted out some great new addition.

"I'm not sure what you think you saw—"

"Tall bloke with dark hair?" Enid finally seemed interested. "Was he handsome beyond all reason?"

"Well, not sure I'd say that," CJ said.

She spun on Bronwen. "It was him again, wasn't it?"

There was no use in lying. She needed to get out in front of this before any more rumors flowed through the troupe. "It was." She held up a hand when Enid made to interrupt her. "I'm in no danger from him, Enid. You'll have to trust me on that count." Turning to CJ, she added, "And he isn't auditioning to be a member of the troupe. I can't really explain what you saw. But it wasn't a trick and I won't ask him to perform. Best for you to forget you ever saw him."

"Not sure I can do that, Bron," he said.

"I'm more than sure you can. You better."

He laughed, not taking her seriously at all.

"This isn't a joke, CJ. He isn't someone to be messed about with. We'll just need to think of some other way to get things back on track."

"So that's it then?" Enid said. "You're all in on whatever game he's playing? Did he at least tell you his real name?"

"There's no game. At least not from him. And yes." Bronwen looked steadily at her sister. "His name is Darkness."

Fifteen

The shadows were everywhere. Hiding behind barrels at dusk, flickering in walkways under the dancing carnival lamps, lurking under wagons in the bright light of day.

In each one, Bronwen saw flickers of memory.

Flickers of Darkness.

She felt as if her mind were constantly playing tricks on her. He was there one moment but gone the next.

It had to be the dreams or memories or whatever it was that was plaguing her. They were getting to the point of obsession. She spent every night willing herself to fall asleep and dream of him, if only to gain another piece of the puzzle, and every waking moment trying to unravel how those puzzle pieces fit together.

If she could see him again, talk to him, maybe he'd help her solve the riddle of her life.

But it wasn't just him she was remembering. It was bits and pieces of her life—or lives, if Enid was to be believed. Pieces that had nothing to do with Darkness were coming back as well.

Her father's funeral. Friendships long gone. New acts. Imagined hurts and real ones. Small disasters and fantastic celebrations. The first train they were able to secure for their travels. Clive and Maggie and a beautiful baby boy saying their farewells as they left to settle into a quiet life of farming. A trip across the sea, taking the carnival to new lands and people. A return trip and feeling as if she were home again, back where she belonged. Fights and torments and cruelties. Sugar and spices and the most delicious things she could imagine. Fear and pain and loneliness.

It was all coming back, and along with these scattered bits of the lives she had lived, she knew two things. First, even if she had moments of happiness in these past decades, she had never lived a happy life. And second, even if she thought there were people who might love her, she had refused to ever be *in* love.

It was a heartbreaking thing to know. But know it she did. Whatever kept her tied to this place, it wasn't love and it wasn't happiness. And it wasn't something she intended to keep her tied down any longer.

She needed to find Darkness to see what else he would be willing to share with her, and she needed to free herself from the carnival for good.

Using a pair of hooks, she pulled and stretched the glob of pale yellow taffy before her. She'd already burned herself twice, her gaze catching imagined movement at just the wrong time.

She didn't even have Tommy for help. He'd been called away to assist with feeding the animals. Before he left she made him promise to stay away from the wagon in the back. She didn't say who was housed inside. She was hopeful CJ would stand by his earlier order that no men were to enter the wagon, but who knew when that order might change. It would be better for Tommy to resign from the troupe than to enter that wagon and meet the same fate as Ty and Rocky, drowned at the bottom of an artificial riverbed.

She spent the next hour cutting and wrapping the candy then decided a walk would help ease the kinks from her neck.

She was almost to the mirror maze when a shadow pulled away from the wooden slat wall ahead of her. It disappeared into the entrance of the maze and she followed.

Mirrors reflect light and images but they also reflect shadows. As she stepped inside, she was immediately surrounded by dim forms and distorted darkness.

Her heart fluttered.

She chased the dark forms from one passage to the next, never quite catching up but thrilled with the chase. Her own face reflected back at her from a myriad of angles. She saw something there she hadn't felt since the morning she'd woken to a different version of herself. Hope and excitement and longing.

The realization made her stumble and collide with the pane in front of her. She righted herself with a grimace as a dark shadow formed in the glass behind her. At least she thought it was behind her.

Darkness. It had to be.

She spun in a slow circle, trying to decide where he was only to be met with more versions of herself.

"I know you're here."

She took a right turn.

"Please. I'd like to talk."

Another few steps forward. Slower now. More cautious.

"If you didn't want me to follow you, why show yourself at all?"

Another left and then a right.

"Thank you. For the stone. It's beautiful."

Another wrong turn. A step back.

A quiet voice in her ear. "Thank you for the sweet."

She jumped and turned, nearly toppling over again. Darkness stood before her. Not a shadow now, but a fully formed man with midnight eyes and onyx hair. His head cocked to one side, the same birdlike gesture from her memory. She knew this man, and not remembering him fully terrified her.

"They're my favorite. But you already knew that, didn't you?" she asked.

"No. I know little about you. Not anymore."

"But you did. I remember that much. You did know me. And I knew you. Before."

He nodded.

"My memories." She pinched the top of her nose, squeezing her eyes tight. "They just . . . stop. Do you know why that is?" She opened her eyes again and was certain he could see the pleading there.

"I do not."

"Do you know how I'm. . ." She waved a hand in front of her face. How does one ask how the hands of time could be turned back so completely?

He studied her as he ran his teeth along his lower lip, deciding what, she couldn't say. "My hope was for you to tell me."

"I know why you're still so handsome." There was no point in denying the fact. Surely he knew how he looked. "Why you've not aged a day. Darkness, son of Carman. It's magic. But I have no magic. I should be. . ." She couldn't say the words.

He said them for her. "Long in the ground."

All the hope, all the excitement, all the longing she'd felt before vanished like sugar on the tongue. Except that wasn't entirely true.

The longing remained.

Longing for the man in front of her.

There was no rational reason for it. She had only just met him again.

Unless. . .

"How long did I know you? In all of these lives I've stolen, were you there? With me?"

He stepped forward and grabbed her wrist. Not hard enough to hurt but she was startled by the contact. "What do you mean lives that you've stolen?"

"I don't know." And she didn't. Not really. But it was what she felt. Something about the whole thing made her feel like a thief, taking something that didn't belong to her. Darkness was right. She should have been long in the ground. She didn't know why she wasn't, but she knew it wasn't right. She told him as much and he listened. He listened, but didn't release her.

"I cannot say what has happened to you, Bronwen, but I mean to find out. The answer to your other question is no. I was not there for any of the in-between."

"How long ago?"

He dropped her wrist and frowned.

"Enid says it's been four lifetimes. In which of those did we meet?"

"More than a century and less than two."

"My actual life then. The one that belonged only to me."

For some reason, that soothed her the tiniest bit.

He raised a hand toward her face but dropped it before he made contact. For the briefest of moments she thought she saw her own longing reflected back at her. Perhaps it was just the mirrors playing tricks.

"I should get back. The ropes will drop soon."

He nodded. Cleared his throat. Shook his head a fraction. "We've a plan."

"A plan?"

"For the river maiden."

Of course. She grimaced. So wrapped up in her own story, she'd completely forgotten the reason he was there in the first place. A girl trapped and held against her will. She added it to her list of sins.

"Of course. I'm sorry. How can I help?'

"If all goes as it should, you'll be in no danger. Only keep your eyes open to anything worrisome. It will take a few more days for things to be set in motion. If you'd be kind enough to give me sign should danger come calling before that time."

They started working their way out of the maze. Darkness took the turns as if he'd designed the place himself. Under the guise of getting lost, she followed behind a close distance. He smelled the same. Woodsmoke and earth.

"What sort of sign?" she asked.

"Could you hang a lamp outside your wagon?"

"Enid might notice. We share it, you know."

He stopped and looked back at her. "Still?"

She smiled. "Still. It seems we are never far from one another's side."

His face went taut, his lips a tight straight line.

Her smile fell. "Did I do something?"

He didn't speak but turned away from her and moved again toward the exit.

"To you? Did I do something to you? Before?"

"Bold of you to ask. If one of us should be wronged, does it not make more sense that I should be the one to inflict such harm upon you?"

In a way she supposed it did, but it didn't feel right to her. Yet she could tell by his posture and the way he'd not look at her she wasn't going to get anything more from him on the subject.

"The board on the confectionary. I can leave a message there. Something no one will suspect. What is your least favorite flavor?"

His shoulders relaxed but he didn't speak.

"Oh. Is that something I should know?" she asked.

He shook his head. "You misunderstand my reaction. Do most know their least favorite?"

"Of course they do. Just as they know which they love the most."

"What are yours?" he asked.

"My favorite is cherry-lime." The tightness left his face, and she smiled in return. "And my least favorite is fig."

"A reasonable choice."

"Thank you."

They were almost to the exit. She really did need to get back to work but was loath for this time between them to end.

"Licorice. It's most vile."

A short laugh burst from her lungs.

"Is that humorous?"

"It's just . . . unexpected."

He stepped out from the wood and glass attraction, and Bronwen marveled at the ease in which he pulled the gloom from the day's light and swaddled himself in it. For anyone watching, it would seem she was all alone under the shadow of a cloud.

For anyone watching, that was, except for the witch Carman.

Sixteen

"Well, isn't this the pretty picture?"

Darkness, safely cocooned inside his shadows, cursed.

"Language, Dub."

Dub. The sound of his name on the air brought a pang to her heart.

Bronwen looked around to see where the melodic voice came from. As she did, she was enveloped in gloom, thick as cotton wool. The sun above her dimmed to night, and the noise of the troupe's daily preparations fell away.

"You think to hide her from me?" the beautiful voice asked.

When she turned back, a woman of such otherworldly beauty stood next to Darkness. Her beautiful bronze hair fell in cascading waves over her equally bronze shoulders. She wore a simple dress of pale cotton, adorned with stitched butterflies along the collar and hem.

"No, Mother. I think to hide us all from them." He pointed, and outside the veil of shadow, Bronwen could make out CJ and the newly youthful Kerb headed their way.

Mother? *This* was Carman?

It all made sense now. The stories. The tales. The warnings.

This woman exuded power. She *was* magic.

"Honestly, Dub. You give me so little credit." Her voice was flippant. "But no mind. Their time will come. I can smell the stench of the thing even from here."

"What are you doing here?" Bronwen didn't miss the way Darkness took a half step in front of her, putting himself between her and the witch.

"Don't you think the better question is what is *she* doing here?"

He didn't move as Carman pointed at her. "It's danced across my mind, yes."

"Oh, for all the stars in this world and the next. I don't plan to do her harm." She smiled at Bronwen. "Yet."

"Hello, I'm Bronwen." Bronwen was smart enough not to insult the witch by ignoring her, but she was also smart enough not to say anything more.

"Lovely girl, I know exactly who you are."

"Oh." Bronwen looked to Darkness. There was no help to be found there. His face was a blank mask.

"Yes. I know you've have a magic all your own." Bronwen's stomach clenched and only relaxed when Carman continued. "Taking sugar and transforming it into something most divine."

"Umm, yes? I suppose you could say that."

"I can and I did." She turned to Darkness. "What I find most intriguing is that I haven't heard about those divine concoctions in quite some time. I'd think it a prudent thing to share, wouldn't you?"

Darkness inhaled through his nose but did not answer.

"Strange the secrets we keep or the lies we tell, even to those we care for. I too have been guilty of it, I suppose."

She turned back to Bronwen, effectively dismissing him from any further conversation. "Tell me, lovely girl, what secrets do you keep? What lies have you told to someone you care for?" Her tone had dropped, and whatever artificial benevolence she had been masquerading behind was gone.

Bronwen was suddenly very uneasy. "I don't know."

"No, I don't believe you do. But I think before this is all over you will. Tell me this, then. Do you know what secret he kept?"

"Mother." Tension thick in that one word.

"No, I don't suppose you know that either. And I can see he'd rather I not share it now. But I will say this. You did me a great service all those years ago, and I never forget a favor."

Carman turned on her heel and left, walking easily out of the gloom and through the camp without a backward glance, leaving Bronwen distinctly confused.

"Remember the signal." With that, Darkness took his shadows and followed his mother out of sight.

Seventeen

BEFORE

Much to Bronwen's delight, Darkness did travel with them. Just not in the way that CJ or the coin counting had hoped.

As they moved from village to town, shore to farmland, he followed along in their wake. Always staying out of sight of the troupe, he'd wait until evening fell and the ropes dropped, doing what exactly, Bronwen couldn't say. Then as the patrons filled the grounds, he would mingle with the gloom and shadows until the carnival closed for the night, only to find Bronwen. They would share a small scrumptious morsel, an hour or two of quiet talk, and a stroll around the quieting camp.

Bronwen looked forward to these visits each time she woke and found a renewed energy as she mixed sugar and magic, butter and dreams into her work. Despite his peculiarities and the reputation that preceded him, she was growing ever more fond of the quiet man.

She thought telling Enid the man she'd been chatting with

was in fact "The Darkness" was going to be difficult, but her sister took hardly any convincing at all. "I knew there was something off with him. Just be careful, Winnie" was all she'd said.

Bronwen had expected more questions, but they hadn't come. Maybe Enid was growing up too. Or maybe she just had her mind on other things.

Bronwen, however, did have questions. How had he become the stuff of nightmares and cautionary tales? She'd seen not an ounce of brutality from him.

Where were his mother and siblings? The feared witch Carman, Violence and Evil.

How long would he stay with her? She worried over that the most.

One night as they walked along the ocean's edge in a town without a name, she dared to voice at least one of those questions.

"Why do the tales always make you sound so wicked?" She rolled the small grey stone he'd given her over and over in her hands.

"Wicked? Do they?" He had his hands clasped behind his back as he strolled along, seeming without a care in the world.

"You must know they do."

"In all the stories I've collected, I'd say they paint Violence and Evil as wicked. I'm more just . . . gloomy."

She stopped walking and looked at him. "Gloomy! Not the stories I've heard. You are, after all, your mother's favorite. Always ready to do her *wicked* bidding."

He'd continued a handful of paces in front of her. At her words, he stopped as well and turned back, still unfazed. "I don't think of my mother as wicked at all. Misunderstood is far more fitting."

"I'll take your word for it. But she is feared, is she not?"

He held out a hand to her, and she closed the distance, taking his as they continued on.

"Yes, and with good reason. Some men, and an equal number of women, *are* wicked. And to those she shows little mercy. So . . . if they're the ones doing the telling, I'd guess they'd label her the mirror of their own. And me and Dother and Dain right alongside her." He said it so matter-of-fact, not the least bit concerned with how he was portrayed.

"That's the first time I've heard you use those names," she said.

"Violence and Evil are more nicknames, I suppose."

"So your brothers, do they then name you Dub?"

He nodded. "Aye."

"And does anyone else use it?"

"Here and there." They walked on in silence for a few minutes more. "You may use it if you like. I'd not be offended."

She wasn't certain why offering her his real name affected her so, but she suddenly felt closer to him than she ever had. Closer than holding his hand as they were now. Closer than trading chocolates for pebbles.

"All right then. Perhaps I shall," she said softly.

"And you, Mistress Sweetling, do you have some other secret name I should know?"

She smiled as she shook her head. "Enid calls me Winnie, but everyone else just sticks with Bronwen or the occasional Bron. But that isn't my favorite."

"Perhaps I shall remedy that one day too. A secret name only I know," he offered.

"Perhaps you should remedy it now. I like the idea of a secret name."

"Does anyone else name you Sweetling?"

She laughed. "No. I can't say that they do."

"Then Sweetling it is."

He pulled her hand where it was still joined with his and brought the knuckles to his lips. It was the first time he'd done such a thing, and she felt the butterflies as they took flight in her stomach.

"Your face was made to smile, Sweetling."

She could hardly breathe, much less answer. "Thank you."

"It's much better than the worry you often wear."

That helped her find her voice. "Believe me, I'd much rather smile all the time."

"You mentioned before your father's a man unafraid to make a wager. Is that why you worry so?"

She nodded slowly. "It's part of it, yes."

"Why? It seems you've a popular carnival, surely many folk pay good coin."

"Yes, they do. But on more than one occasion, those coins haven't made it into the hands that they should. Rather than paying the troupe, well. . ." She once again found it hard to continue, but this time for a very different reason.

"It is gambled away," he finished for her.

She nodded.

"And because it's your father's troupe, it's also yours. You feel you must atone for his mistakes." It wasn't a question, but a statement of understanding.

"That might be a bit of a dark way to put it, but yes. I suppose that's fairly accurate."

"Darkness is as shadows do. I cannot change, or perhaps I choose not too." His voice had taken on the odd singsong quality it sometimes did. It was another thing about him she didn't understand. It didn't bother her, but she wanted to know what caused the alteration in him.

"Why do you talk that way some of the time but not all of the time?" she asked.

He tilted his head, black eyes boring into her. That bird-like quality back again.

"I've been raised by a woman who makes nothing plain. It was always riddles and guessing and testing when I was young. I've tried to dampen it, but old habits win out on occasion. The more I'm with you, the better it gets. But sometimes . . . I slip."

She didn't want him to feel bad about who he was. "I don't mind it. It makes you unique."

"When I've spent a time with my family, I have to fight to break it."

"Don't fight yourself over me."

"I'd fight more than myself over you, Sweetling." He kissed her knuckles once more, and she felt breathless all over again. "How might you go about it?"

It took her a moment to recall what he was referring to.

"CJ says I need a great act. Something fey even. One to draw in the crowds. I argued with him. Told him fey weren't real." She grimaced. "Obviously I was mistaken."

"Obviously."

"But even in my error, I stand by my position. I hardly think it fair to employ someone with that sort of magic. It should be for them to use as they wish, not as some silly carnival trick and certainly not to give my father more coins to simply throw away." She paused and took a deep breath. "Sorry, that was probably more than you cared to hear."

"I care very much to hear whatever you'd like to share with me, Sweetling."

She smiled her thanks. "He saw you that night. When you convinced me with your shadows. Thought you were the 'new act.'" She gave him a sheepish look.

"As you suggest, I prefer my space. Out of sight." Bronwen couldn't have anticipated his next words and was thankful he said them with something like teasing in his voice. "I suppose if you asked it of me, I'd do it. Just to see you smile."

"That's not a very good trade."

"For me it is. There is nothing you could ask of me that I would refuse." Now he sounded completely serious. It made her chest ache. "No questions. No arguments. I'd do it. You only need utter the words."

The idea was so absurd, she couldn't help but release a nervous laugh. "You shouldn't make promises like that. One day someone might take you up on it."

"And that would be bad?"

"Of course it would be bad. Even the ones we love the most need a bit of a fight every now and then. Otherwise, it just seems you don't really care."

"I'd not thought of it that way. I still offer it as a promise to you. If you ever have need for me to, I vow it."

"I'll keep that in mind." She smiled at him and returned to their earlier subject. "I'm no performer either. I don't even tell people I'm the hands behind the candies."

"Even if you were to find a way to bring larger crowds, would that not be simply a larger pot for the gambling?"

"That is exactly the problem. I have no solution."

"This CJ. Has he a stake in it all?"

Odd that he chose CJ to comment on. Not Enid or any of the others.

"In one way or another, we all do. But CJ has been with us since we were kids. He's almost like a brother. He's got no people. Not anymore. If something were to happen to the show, I'm not sure what he'd do."

They'd circled the outside of the camp twice already, but Bronwen had no desire to return to her wagon. For one thing, it would be the end of her time with Darkness—she couldn't bring herself to call him Dub just yet. And for another, Enid would be there waiting. She had made it clear she wasn't a fan of the time Bronwen had been spending with Darkness, even if she accepted who he was. She'd even gone so far as to threaten telling their father about it.

It wasn't as if Bronwen were a child. She was old enough to make her own choices, but she wasn't ready to acknowledge exactly where those choices might lead.

Darkness had the uncanny ability to sense her thoughts and often didn't hold back from his observations. "You could leave it to your father and this CJ, you know. Let him have the weight of the worries."

"I could."

"You could make confections anywhere."

She didn't like the sound of that. "I could, but why would I?"

"You could make them for me? Come with me, I mean. Leave the worries?" He rarely sounded unsure, but in that moment, he did.

Bronwen stopped walking. Had he just said what she thought? Asked her to leave the carnival for him?

"I . . . I don't really know. . ." Her breath was coming too quickly. Short rapid bursts that had her heart racing to keep up. She wasn't sure if it was the idea of leaving the carnival behind or the idea that he wanted her to. Was she scared or thrilled?

Both.

"Oh, Sweetling. Calm. I didn't mean to—"

"It's all right," she cut him off. "I'm all right. I just . . . what are you asking?"

He stepped to her and put a hand on either side of her face, tilting it up to meet his dark eyes. "Calm first."

"I am calm."

"No. You are not."

"I am calm. What are you asking me?"

"For you. For you to be with me. Always."

He traced a thumb over her lower lip. "In all of my long years on this earth, I've never felt so akin to anyone. Not my mother, though I respect her. Not my brothers, though for them I would die. I've found women attractive, but I haven't felt more than a passing fancy."

"Well, maybe don't share that bit with me just now," she said to lighten things a touch.

He didn't smile as she'd hoped he would, just studied her face. "Now I feel this thing. Longing? Exquisite pain? An irrational desire to wrap myself in you and not let go. I envision us together every moment of the day and night. I dream of you, Bronwen. I can't remember ever dreaming of anyone before. I don't want it to end."

It was such a lot to take in. She knew she should respond with some grand declaration. She spoke the only words she could think of. "Neither do I. Want it to end, I mean."

Before the words were out of her mouth, he bent and brushed his lips over hers.

If night were a flavor, she tasted it on her lips. Dark and lush and full of hidden promises.

"So you will?" he asked.

She wanted so badly to say yes.

But . . . she couldn't.

He must have read it in her face. "I see I've misjudged your feelings."

"You haven't. Not at all. You're all I think of too. I think. . ."

"You think what, Sweetling?"

"I think I may be in love with you?"

"You ask it like a question. Do you not know the answer?" His voice was pained.

"Yes. No, I do. It's just . . . I can't leave. Just like that. Not now."

"Ever?"

She thought about that. Could she leave eventually? Yes. Did she want to? Also yes. She never would have thought that would be the case. She loved the circuit. Loved her father and

Enid. But it wasn't an easy life. She longed to be settled somewhere one day. In a small cottage with an enormous kitchen. A place of safety and refuge.

And someone to share it with. And yes. She did love him.

She just didn't know if Darkness would be able to provide that safe warm place for her. He was, after all, a thing of myth and folklore. The monster under the bed and in the shadows. There was a reason for the stories, even if it seemed so foreign to the man she'd come to love.

And then she knew. Deep in her heart she knew he would. He would do anything she asked and more.

"I think so. I just need to find the right time. I can't leave them like this. I need to know they'll be all right."

He nodded.

With an earnestness that melted her heart as easily as sugar in water, he asked, "And what of you? You have not a care for your own well being?"

"No. I care. And I trust you." She clasped his hands in hers, bringing them to her face so she could kiss the inside of his wrist. "How will you explain it to your family?"

"There is nothing to explain. They aren't as bad as you suppose. If I say you make me happy, they'll be happy with me."

"But you're Darkness?"

"Yes. I will continue to be Darkness." He smiled as he ran his thumb over her lower lip again. "But even in the dead of night, it takes light to bring the shadows. You can be my light, Bronwen."

Eighteen

Bronwen woke in a cold sweat and immediately ran to the door, throwing it open just in time to vomit onto the grass beside the steps.

"Shut the door, Winnie, I'm trying to sleep." Enid, unaware of the memories that had come flooding into Bronwen, likely thought her sister was up early for no reason.

"In a minute, Enid." She gulped down air right along with her tears.

When she was sure she wasn't going to be sick again, she closed the door and grabbed the pitcher from beside her bed, careful not to make too much noise, lest Enid scold her from her side of the partition again. She rinsed her mouth and spat into the basin.

You can be my light, Bronwen.

The memory of those words bit into her with a thousand needle-sharp teeth.

He had loved her. And she had loved him. Completely. With her whole heart.

What had happened? Had he left her for another? She was certain nothing in this life or any other would have made her leave someone like him. It had to be why she was so steadfast in her vow to never fall in love.

In snips and bits, she could see he was everything she could ever ask for. Even now she could see it. The blanks in her memory had never been more frustrating. More than frustrating. She was angry. Angry at whatever had caused this lapse in memory. Angry at herself for not knowing what to do about it.

She'd asked him if she'd done something in the past, and he'd so smoothly evaded the question. So maybe she was just the smallest bit angry with him as well for also keeping her past from her.

She needed air.

Or maybe she needed Darkness.

She was unlikely to find either in her wagon, so she grabbed a wrap, slid on her boots, and went out into the early dawn.

Moisture still clung to the grass and the birds were beginning to wake. The troupe still slumbered. She loved this time of day. When all was quiet and still. When there weren't any patrons clamoring for excitement or running headlong toward thrills. No loud music. No glaring lights. No animal cries or crowd exclamations. It was peaceful.

She wanted peaceful.

She was terrified she would never have it.

Even between show days, they broke down camp and moved along, staying up late into the night and sleeping half the day. She was tired of it. Weary and worn.

She knew there had been a time when she'd loved this life on the road, but more and more she was beginning to think that hadn't been so for a long while.

She made a beeline for the backside of the site, hoping to slip out and away from the tents and wagons before most of the troupe woke. She wasn't intentionally headed toward the river maiden's wagon. At least that's what she told herself.

It couldn't hurt to make sure the girl was still safe. Or better yet, perhaps her rescue mission had come in the night and one less worry would be hanging over Bronwen's head.

As she drew closer, the early morning quiet was disturbed by low voices.

Saints and sinners. Was she to have nothing simple?

She ducked behind the neighboring tent, hoping they'd move along and she could continue her walk.

"It's going to have to be tonight. I'm running out of time." That was CJ's voice.

"Are you sure, boss? Seems a bit of a waste." And Kerb.

"Says the man who got his turn a few nights back."

Bronwen poked her head out to see if they were moving in her direction. They stood just outside the river wagon.

"You know what I mean," Kerb argued. "She hasn't had the chance to warm to us. She might make us money yet."

"It has to be tonight." CJ pulled a handkerchief from his waistcoat pocket and coughed into it. The pitying look on Kerb's face told her all she needed to know about what the dark splatters on it were. "The last stragglers of the new troupe's gotten suspicious enough after you and the girls. It's our last show here in Feyport. You can give the rest of 'em the deal or not and we can pick up new hands when we land down the coast later this week. That close to the city, there's always crew looking to get set up."

"I get all that, but why the girl? Let's look for another clod tonight."

"You think I haven't looked. I planned this stop for just that reason. Feyport was meant to be crawling with fey. The juice from any one of them would last me forever. I'd never need to take another ride."

Bronwen's breathing quickened. CJ had to be talking about his trick to gain back the years time added to them all.

"All right. All right," Kerb placated him. "We'll need to have the girls help us out. She won't go without a fight."

"I'll see that they do. You just make sure the place gets cleared out early. Soon as that's done, meet us in the back."

Kerb didn't look happy, but he nodded.

Bronwen didn't know what exactly they were talking about, but it didn't sound like she had much of a choice. She needed to let Darkness know their time was nearly up.

Her walk forgotten, she waited until CJ and Kerb had moved along. Then she headed to the sweets wagon, grabbed her chalk, and with a shaking hand adjusted the offerings menu. At the top in blocky bold letters, she wrote:

SPECIAL

ONE NIGHT ONLY

MIDNIGHT LICORICE

She returned to her wagon. Enid was still softly snoring.

Bronwen lay down and closed her eyes. In her dreams, Darkness was waiting.

Nineteen

Bronwen lay on the riverbank, a blanket spread out around her. Beside her a picnic box was overflowing with small sandwiches, apples, a bottle of honeyed mead, and a dozen different cakes she'd brought along so Darkness could taste them all. He bit into the last one, a wicked smile on his face. Damson plum jam squished out between his fingers and onto his chin. Bronwen leaned up on one elbow and smiled as she wiped the jam off with her thumb. Before she could lie back down, Darkness snatched at her wrist. A laugh bubbled up from her belly. He took her thumb between his lips and sucked the jam clean from her skin. The laughter died as quickly as it had come, replaced by a contented sigh.

Twenty

Bronwen stood in front of the character cutouts, wooden planks adorned with comical characters in various ridiculous poses. Each had round ovals cut into the characters, giving just enough space for patrons to stick their faces through to entertain their friends.

Her favorite was a man with a comically large chest and teeny tiny legs. He wore a dotted waistcoat in a garish shade of orange and purple striped trousers. Beside him a dog was standing on its hind legs, pink bow around its neck.

Without a thought, she ducked behind it and stuck her face through the hole, becoming the comical man. Darkness frowned at her.

"What? You don't like how I look?"

"No. I love how you look."

"Oh." Her face flushed, and she stepped back from the plank. "Well, I love how you look too."

Twenty-one

BEFORE

Her father cursed as he picked up the broken shards of glass from in front of one of their best attractions. "This glass will cost a fortune to replace. We'll need to close it down until I can get to the city for a new mirror."

"Can't we just adjust the maze? Take the broken panel out?" she asked.

"If you think you can configure the thing better, be my guest." He was getting testier every time she spoke to him. If he could just control himself and keep the money from flying out of his pockets, one broken mirror wouldn't be the end of things.

She knew him though. Perhaps better than he knew himself. He just couldn't help thinking he'd win it all back. He never did. Over and over and over again. Digging them deeper and deeper.

She wiped the frustrated tears from her eyes and went into the maze, looking for a way to salvage the attraction.

A moment later, a shadow followed her in.

"Sweetling? How can I help?"

She shook her head, not meeting his gaze. She'd never felt quite so ashamed of her father, not even when she was telling the troupe there were no wages to be had. This was different. She'd turned down Darkness's offer to leave so she could fix this mess and she was failing. So maybe it wasn't her father she was so ashamed of.

"This isn't your worry."

"Your worries are mine."

She knew he was behind her, but when she raised her eyes, it was his gaze she met in the mirrors. The moment she looked at him, she broke down again.

He opened his arms and held her while she cried. Kissed the top of her head.

After she collected herself, he moved the broken frame, and together they made a new path that was better than the last.

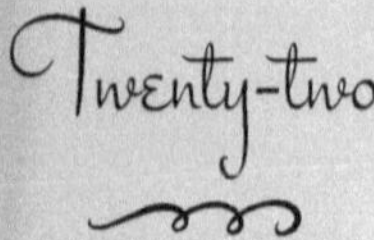

Twenty-two

BEFORE

The crowd was thin that night. Bronwen did all she could to sell as many treats as possible, but this far north, most of the patrons preferred savory mutton pies and strong fish stews. Neither of those were on her list of confections. The best she could do was warmed chocolate melted into frothy sweet milk, a handmade marshmallow floating at the surface.

She twiddled her hair and watched as small groups of families and occasional couples ambled past her pink and white wagon without a second look.

She was just about to give up and shutter the wagon for the night when a beautiful woman with a gleaming smile and a man built to slay armies walked up to the window. He had hair the color of a winter's snow and eyes that twinkled in the lamps.

"I hear you make the most wonderful treats," the woman said. "We'll take one of each please."

"One of . . . everything?" No one could eat one of everything. "Are you sure?"

"Absolutely, lovely girl. Absolutely."

They gave her a mountain of coins, and she filled several paper bags with an assortment of goodies. As she was handing them over, she saw a man with hair of fire watching from the tree line.

Twenty-three

BEFORE

Darkness pulled her hair to the side and kissed her neck.

"I've no stone for you today."

"I don't need the stones. I only need you."

<h1 style="text-align:center">Twenty-four</h1>

BEFORE

Her father was dead.

In truth, Alfie Elwell had been dead for a long time. On the inside at least. No happiness or joy. Each day a struggle.

Finally, he could be at peace. That's what she told herself. One day she would be at peace too.

Twenty-five

BEFORE AND BEFORE AND BEFORE AND AGAIN

"This is so tiresome, Winnie. Get on the damned carousel. Over and over we've done this. And you fight every time."

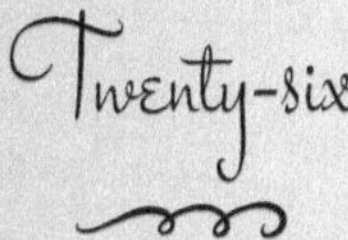

It was dark in the wagon.

Dark and murky and cool.

The camp wasn't fully quiet. A few attractions were still up and running, but she'd closed for the night. In hindsight, she should have just told CJ she was unwell and shuttered the sweets wagon, but she didn't want to give him any reason to suspect things were amiss.

But her distraction was evident. Another night brimming with unease and the growing sense of wrongness. More than just a tad off.

After waking from her nap with so many new memories, she could barely stand to be in her own skin. She was still missing pieces, but the puzzle was nearing completion, and she didn't care for the image it formed.

She had been so happy with Darkness. Until she wasn't.

Why? She didn't know.

She no longer felt like the troupe was her family. She didn't belong here. Not any longer.

How many times had she felt just this way, ready to run? She didn't know.

How many times had she been kept from running? She didn't know.

She didn't know. She didn't know. She didn't know.

But she was going to find out.

Those answers would have to wait. She had something more important to do first.

If she was quick, she might be able to loosen Neeve's ropes. Might be able to give her a chance to get out on her own. She'd wait for whatever plan Darkness had set in motion if she had to, but she would rather this be done sooner than later. What if he hadn't seen her sign? What if he'd been called to some other task?

She wanted the water maiden free because it was the right thing to do, but she also wanted her free so Bronwen could find freedom of her own.

It was easy to get inside, no one standing guard or keeping watch. Just a handpainted sign out front with the words "Attraction Closed" in the same crisp font labeling several other attractions. Just a slipknot of rope latched the door on the outside. Nothing to see here.

She eased the door open and peered into the gloom.

"Hello?" she whispered into the dark, afraid of lighting a lamp and drawing attention to the wagon.

The soft sloshing of water was the only reply.

She slid the rest of the way into the wagon and left the door cracked behind her. If someone noticed anything, she'd say she heard a noise and came to investigate. The fact that the river wagon was on the opposite side of the camp from her own was problematic, but she'd worry about a story later. Her biggest risk was Enid and a few other women being sent to fetch the water maiden for whatever horror CJ had planned. If that happened, she'd lie and tell them he'd asked her to help.

"Hello?" Another whisper. Another slosh of water.

"Are you there? Neeve?"

Slosh. Slosh. Slosh.

Hands stretched out in front of her, Bronwen ventured farther into the wagon.

Slosh. Slosh. Slosh.

"I'm here to help you."

Another step forward. She could smell the water. Dark and dank and full of malice.

Slosh.

The door behind her creaked. She spun around and stepped back, colliding with a smooth solid surface. The tank.

She felt the splash of water as a hand grabbed her upper arm.

She yelped at the contact.

Above her a woman hissed. In front of her a man cursed.

With the sound of glass shattering, she was yanked to the side as a torrent of water flooded the space, threatening to take her feet from under her. And then she was being hauled up into arms far too powerful.

"Let's go, ladies."

It was madness. Coming from a woman raised in the carnival, fairly certain she had been party to some variety of dark magic, and just as certain she had been in love with the embodiment of darkness itself, that was saying something.

Water rolled out of the wagon in diminishing waves. Kicked up from the man who carried her in his arms, it splashed up and soaked the bottom of her trousers. An unholy yowling was coming from behind her. It had to be Neeve. Lamps that had been winking off earlier were flickering back to life all over camp. Shouts dotted the night.

"You can put me down," Bronwen seethed. "I'm on your side. I think."

It was hard to declare a side when she wasn't entirely sure who it was carrying her. The flowing white hair led her to believe it was Violence.

"Nothing to do with sides, lovely. I can move faster than you," the man replied.

"Why do I need to move fast?"

The yowling behind them turned to a string of cursing that would make a showman blush. It was answered by another man's deep voice, slightly breathless and providing an equally colorful reply.

"You smell like the sea," Neeve moaned. Whether in disgust or elation, Bronwen couldn't say. "Why do you smell like the sea?"

"That'll be the selkie." The other man sounded not at all impressed with her.

So there were selkies in Feyport. Enid would be thrilled.

She tried to twist about in her captor's arms to get a glimpse of what was happening a handful of yards behind. She wanted to see the selkie for herself. An unfamiliar man with gold and silver hair was struggling with a writhing mess of wet limbs and sodden material.

The water maiden was doing her best to wriggle from the man's arms.

She was drawn back to their flight when her captor—rescuer?—asked, "You weren't meant to be in that wagon, were you?"

"Well, no, but if you drop me now, no one will be the wiser."

"That crow has called, lovely."

She pulled her eyes from the pair behind them and realized he was right. Several showmen, Kerb included, were headed directly for them.

"Just put me down and get her out of here. I'll be fine."

"If I put you down, I will be forced to act as my nature sees fit. Now please, I'm attempting to save you."

"You are Violence then," she said.

"In name and in nature."

"Well, Violence, I'm not some damsel in need of saving."

"Neither am I," screamed the woman behind them.

"Beg to differ," panted the man carrying the water maiden. This caused her to scream even louder.

"Regretting that deal yet?" Violence called back in a merry tone.

"Tell Darkness I said thank you." With those words, Bronwen surprised Violence by twisting and pushing away from his chest.

He grunted as the movement tripped him up. He let her go, and she was just able to keep her footing as he pulled up short.

Violence chuckled. "Perhaps you could tell him yourself."

That wasn't in her cards. The plan was simple. Get to her wagon. Grab the bag she'd packed earlier in the day when Enid was in the big top rehearsing for her show. Get out of the camp. She had enough money to get her to the city, and from there it was only a matter of time before she could find a job in a sweet shop. She could melt away and grow old there, spending every day of her life attempting to atone for all the years she'd been given at the expense of others. It was a simple plan.

She wasn't sure if he would try to grab her again, so she set off running as soon as her feet hit the ground.

"A little help would be appreciated," the second man said.

Bronwen looked over her shoulder and saw Violence tip her a small salute before turning to help his associate with the struggling water maiden.

They were going to have their hands full it seemed. She

only hoped the girl would allow them to get her far enough away from the camp before they were able to let her go on her own.

Now she just needed to disappear.

The thought was a bitter one. She couldn't say she would miss this life, but there were parts she was fond of. Her pink and white wagon. Enid on the high rope. The smell of sugar in the open night air. Tommy and his quiet company. The feel of taffy on the hook. Children smiling and begging their parents for just one more lolly. The excited roar after a perfectly timed trick. The screams of delighted fright at a perfectly timed jump. Enid pouring her coffee in the quiet early morning. The beautiful multicolored glass that twinkled with the carnival's lamps. The excitement of the rope drop each night. The sound of the calliope. Enid flirting with everyone she saw. Enid on the other side of the partition, falling asleep as she told Bronwen whether or not they'd flirted back.

Enid.

It always came back to her sister. The fun-loving girl on the high wire. The sister she could never leave. The woman who knew what Bronwen didn't.

This is so tiresome, Winnie. Get on the damned carousel. Over and over we've done this. And you fight every time.

She might not ever get the answers she wanted, but it no longer mattered. This time she was leaving and never looking back.

And then there was Darkness. She still didn't know what had happened between them, and though it made her a coward, she was afraid to find out.

With the water maiden and her rescuers far behind, she calmed her breath and her steps. Kerb would undoubtedly be telling CJ about the escape by now. That should keep them all busy enough for the time being. She didn't need more than a minute or two to grab her things. By the time the dust calmed and they came looking for her, she would already be gone.

The wagon was quiet when she let herself in. Her bag was right where she'd left it.

She thought about leaving Enid a note, but what would she say? She'd already told her sister she was thinking of leaving. Enid was a smart girl. She'd either know why Bronwen needed to do this or she wouldn't. Maybe in time she would even understand.

"I love you, Enid." She whispered the words to the empty wagon and hoisted her bag onto her shoulder.

"Not enough it seems."

Bronwen jumped. "Saints and sinners, Enid. You scared the life out of me."

Enid sat reclined on the settee, alone in the dark. "Hmm. Well. . ."

"What are you doing here in the dark?" Bronwen asked.

"I'd ask you the same thing, but it seems pretty obvious."

Bronwen didn't have it in her to argue. "You know I can't stay. This isn't right. Whatever you did? Whatever I did? It isn't right."

"Right or wrong, what's done is done." Enid didn't sound happy or contrite, or anything really. It was as if she were simply reading a grocery list. "But don't worry. If it makes you feel any better, you didn't go willingly."

"What do you mean?"

"Put up a fight each and every time. Every time I was fool enough to think it would be different. That you'd finally learned to appreciate the gift you were given. But nope." She turned down her lips as she shook her head. "I always had to go first so I'd be strong enough to help them get you on the damned thing."

The coolness in her voice sent a shiver down Bronwen's spine.

"What thing?" she demanded, needing to know.

Enid seemed all too happy to tell her. "The carousel, of course. Well to be fair, it wasn't the same carousel all those years ago. Just that rickety little ride Da scrapped together. But you'd fight it each and every time. CJ says that's why you don't remember anything. You fight it so much, it's like your mind refuses to keep it in there."

Dread was filling Bronwen. She knew she'd loathed the horrific ride, and now she understood why. It had been the dark magic that had given her back her youth. But at what cost?

The water maiden. CJ had wanted to use the water maiden tonight. How?

"I fight because I don't want this. It's not right. We are not right."

"Ugh. Winnie, honestly." Enid finally had some passion in her words. "I wish persuading you to embrace this was as easy as persuading you to get rid of Darkness all those years ago."

Bronwen's stomach plummeted. "What did you just say?"

"And now here he is. Back again. Is that why you're sneaking out in the night? Hoping to undo what you did lifetimes ago?" Enid asked.

"No. I just. . ." It was like falling. The memories came hard and fast and all at once Bronwen knew.

She remembered it all.

And she despised herself more than she'd ever despised another person in her life.

Twenty-seven

BEFORE

Darkness was patient.

Weeks went by and still Bronwen struggled with the weight of keeping Elwell & Sons from falling apart.

Her father was able to rig the new ride so it was at least functional. She had to admit the design was quite clever. He fixed the horses on a wooden wheel and attached thick ropes painted in bright colors. A towering pole stretched above the wheel, and the ropes were tethered to the top, overlapping not unlike a maypole. After the patrons were seated on the horses, two of the crew grabbed hold and turned the horses in a circle until the ropes were wound around the pole. When they let go, the ride would unspool itself, sending the horses spinning in a circle. The crowds really did seem to enjoy it.

But even as the crowd continued to show up, the more coins they collected, the worse her father's gambling got. He was chasing debts with no hope of catching up. More and more mornings arrived with nothing to hand out to the troupe. One of the acts had already absconded—the sword swallower, a crowd favorite.

If things didn't turn around soon, Bronwen wouldn't have to worry about leaving the carnival in trouble; it would already be destroyed and she would be free to go wherever Darkness wished to take her.

And even though she couldn't tell him she was ready to run away with him just yet, Darkness still didn't pressure her.

It was this patience that might have doomed them.

Enid was in a foul mood when she dropped onto the bench next to Bronwen one morning.

"The tea is cold," she groused.

"That's what happens when you sleep the day away," Bronwen replied, not unkindly.

"I'd have thought you'd still be in bed yourself." The words were distorted by Enid's yawn. "Seems you never get to bed early anymore."

"I don't see how that's any concern of yours."

"I'm your sister. Plus we share a wagon. Of course it's my concern. He's here every night. I'd have thought he'd lose interest by now. "

Bronwen pulled back, eyes wide. "Wow. I know I'm not the beauty you are, but that stings a bit."

"That's not what I mean." Enid took a large bite of the sweet brown bread in her hand. "It's just, surely you've told him by now you aren't interested in anything more than a passing tryst."

"Enid! Why would you say that?"

"Come on, Winnie. Really? You know you'll never leave Da and me." She tore off another piece of bread and dipped it in her cup.

Bronwen sipped her tea but didn't answer.

"Wait. You aren't thinking of leaving?" Enid slammed her mug down. "Winnie?"

"I'm not going anywhere right now." Bronwen was trying to be placating but knew she was failing. "Don't fret."

"Right now? So you are thinking about it?"

"Eventually. Maybe."

"Winnie." Enid stood up abruptly. "No. That's insane."

Bronwen rolled her eyes. "That's a bit dramatic, don't you think."

"Not at all. How do you expect that to work?"

"What do you mean?"

"Saints and sinners. Leave it to you not to have thought about any of this. He's Darkness, Winnie. Forget the whole 'he does his mother's evil bidding bit.'"

"That isn't true. If you knew him like I do, you wouldn't believe any of that," Bronwen cut in.

"You can believe whatever you like. I'm not done. Darkness has roamed the earth with that family of his for ages. And he looks no older than you? Clearly there's some big magic at work. Magic, I will remind you, you didn't even believe in six months ago. Magic that will continue to work for years to come, no doubt. "

"What's your point?" Bronwen asked.

"My point? Jeez, Winnie. My point is last time I checked, you don't have that sort of magic. Are you following now? He will not age."

Bronwen felt herself go ever so slightly sideways. "But I will. I'll age and he'll stay just as he is."

The truth of it hit Bronwen with all the force of a sledge. She'd questioned it of course. Briefly. But then she'd put it from her mind and refused to even think about what it might mean. She refused to believe he was the bringer of bad things the stories said, but now she wondered what else she wasn't considering. She'd been so caught up in the way he made her feel. Caught up in the fact that he'd picked her, of all the women he'd come in contact with before. Caught up in the ease she felt at his side and the escape he could promise. Caught up and not seeing. And in doing so, she'd let herself forget about all the other warnings she should have been paying attention to.

"I know you feel something for him, Winnie. If you didn't, you wouldn't have that look of complete and utter despair you're wearing right now. But just think it through. Don't make any big decisions yet."

Bronwen could barely look at her sister. "Nothing's decided."

"I only want your happiness, Winnie. You know that."

Bronwen smiled at her sister, but even she knew it was the sort of smile that held sadness in the curve of her lips.

That evening Darkness didn't meet her outside the confection wagon, and she wondered if he somehow sensed the doubt Enid had so effectively sown in her mind.

Nor did he leave her a stone. Perhaps it was for the best, though it certainly didn't feel that way.

She'd steeled herself to ask him all the things she'd been avoiding. Tell him how she truly felt and hope there was a way for them to move forward. She wasn't fool enough to pretend she didn't love him with every fiber of her being, but she knew she would do what was right for both of them. If that meant breaking her own heart to prevent him breaking it later, she'd do what needed to be done.

It was two days before she saw him again, and by that time, running away with him was the last thing on her mind.

The night started out just as any other. The stalls were busy, the patrons happy, and the caramel apples selling well.

She'd somehow misplaced the metal tongs she favored

when serving up the particularly sticky treats, so she had been reduced to using one hand for the confections and the other to exchange coins. It slowed her down, but only marginally.

An hour or two after the ropes dropped, she was handing over a cone of candy floss when her father came barreling up the alley to her wagon. He was closely followed by CJ, and both men looked as if trouble chased on their heels.

She still had a line at the window, but her father came round the back and up the steps.

"Bronwen, I need you to close up and go fetch Enid," he said without preamble.

"Alfie, I told you that wasn't necessary right now," CJ said.

"What's going on?" Bronwen asked.

"There's been some trouble stirred up." Her father looked more weary than she'd ever seen him. "Fetch your sister and meet us back here."

"What sort of trouble?"

"The bad sort. Now go," CJ answered for him.

She glared at him.

"Sorry, Bronwen." CJ softened his voice, but not enough for her liking. "Just go fetch Enid. We all need to talk." It sounded like an order. Since when did he think he could order her about? But her father could, and he'd demanded the same thing.

Bronwen apologized to the line of guests waiting for treats and shuttered the window. She grabbed the coins from her till and shoved them into a pocket and headed to the show tent, hastily wiping her hands on her apron as she went.

She was perturbed with the way CJ had spoken to her and that her father hadn't stood up to him on her behalf—hadn't even bothered to answer her question at all.

It didn't take long to reach the tent. Enid was backstage wiping her face. She must have just finished her act and would be taking a break before putting on the second of the night.

"Da needs to talk to us, and before you ask I have no idea what's going on."

"Its likely to do with the brawl earlier," Enid said.

"What brawl?"

"Bunch of local lads were in the curiosity tent and the lamps all went out. They got a bit rowdy, and the fellas had to escort them out. It turned into a whole mess."

"Why didn't I hear about it?"

"No idea. Let's go see what Da's on about, then."

They made it back to the wagon at the same time as some of the troupe who kept things in line for the shows.

None of them looked happy.

They'd cornered Bronwen's father up against the side of the pink and white wagon. At least the patrons had been shooed away and wouldn't be there to witness whatever was about to happen.

"Now, Alfie, you can't expect us to continue on like this," Kerb said. "And tonight Gibby was hurt. Got cornered and those lads took their ire out on him before we broke it all up."

Gibby was one of the older troupe members. He'd been with them for years. Generally he was tasked with taking tickets, but he also helped out wrangling the crowd if it got out of hand. He had a gentle soul but the voice of a cranky demon.

Brownen's heart hurt to think he'd been injured.

"Well now, lads, it's not all that bad. I've been paying you what I could," her father said.

Kerb sighed. "Which isn't more than a drop of piss in the ocean."

Her father wouldn't be silenced. "And what happened with Gibby wasn't good, I'll admit that, but it happens from time to time."

"It wouldn't have happened if we'd been fully manned, Alfie. We were short and you know why."

Bronwen's face fell. He hadn't allowed her to continue

collecting the take and paying out, and now it seemed they were in straits again. Who hadn't been working? She didn't know. But if lack of wages had anything to do with it, they were in worse trouble than she thought.

Bronwen walked up and stood next to her father. "Is this true? Have they not been paid?"

"That's not important right now," CJ said. "Did you lot get those troublemakers out of here?"

"Oh, aye. They're gone," Kerb said.

"Good. I don't know what got them so riled up to start."

"It was when the wind came through and the lamps went out. Said we were pulling some kind of fast one on 'em. I think they'd all just had a spot too much of the whiskey before they made their way in."

"Right then." CJ looked at the men around him. "We need to get the show up and going again. Gibby'll be fine. He's a tough buzzard. I want any sign of trouble directed to me. Everyone clear on that?"

"No. Not clear on that at all," Bronwen said.

"Alfie can explain it all in a minute. I wanted him to wait, but seems he's got a burr up his arse."

"CJ!" She was shocked to hear him talk about her father that way. He'd been like family, and even if they disagreed, he'd always respected her da.

"Fine. We can discuss this all later." Again her father had that broken look about him. "Girls, go on back to work. We can meet at your wagon when the show's done."

He walked away from them, not toward the center of the carnival but out the back as if he had no plans of getting himself back to work beside the rest of them.

She turned to CJ. "What's this all about?"

"You should hear it from him."

"Really? That's all you're going to say?" she demanded.

"It is."

"Enid, do you know what's going on?" Bronwen asked.

"Not any more than you do."

"Well what about this trouble then?" Bronwen turned back to CJ. "You going to tell us what that was all about?"

"Maybe you should ask your friend instead." His tone was bitter but also maybe just the littlest bit smug. She didn't care for it.

"My friend?"

"Saints and sinners. As if we needed anything more to add to the night." Enid rolled her eyes and crossed her arms, tipping her head toward the back of the wagon.

Bronwen turned where she'd indicated and saw Darkness standing behind the steps.

A tiny thrill ran through her at the sight of him.

He was just as mesmerizing as he'd always been to her. Just as handsome. Just as calm.

When he looked at her, one eyebrow cocked in question, she knew he saw her. Saw that she was desperately confused and a little hurt. Not by him exactly, though he had a part in it.

"Enid, you've got a show to do." Bronwen's attention snapped back to CJ. She didn't like his tone at all. A chill ran down her spine.

"Don't speak to her that way," Bronwen warned him.

"I don't know what's going on here," Enid said, not rising to CJ's bait, "but you're right. I've got a show. See you later, Winnie."

"You should get back to work too."

Bronwen ignored CJ as she walked over to where Darkness was waiting. He hadn't gotten involved in the conversation, and she silently thanked him for that.

"Sweetling, you are distressed."

"Yes." She shook her head and smiled. "But you're here. That's good."

"Is it?" He tilted his head again. It was the look he wore when he was puzzling something out.

"Yes." She didn't elaborate.

"I'm sorry I didn't tell you I might miss our evening walk. I had a matter to discuss with my mother."

There's been some trouble. It was when the wind came through and the lamps went out. Why don't you ask your friend?

Surely she was being ridiculous. There was no reason to suspect Darkness had anything to do with the evening's events.

"Oh?"

"Will you walk with me?"

She nodded, and he took her hand, pulling her closer to the edge of the site.

"Have you given any more thought to the idea of coming with me?"

She hadn't expected that. They hadn't discussed it again since he'd asked weeks before. But that didn't mean she hadn't been thinking about it. She had. Endlessly. Until about an hour ago.

"I have." She chewed at her lower lip. Could she tell him she wanted to leave right then and there? Could she tell him she had her doubts? Would he help her decide or be hurt by the confession?

"Before you say more, I'd like to give you something."

"Oh?"

She expected him to pull out a ring or a locket or a brooch. Something to signify his love for her. A token to tell others she was spoken for.

It wasn't a ring or a locket or a brooch that he pulled from his waistcoat pocket.

It was a small sachet, no larger than a plum and just as deep a damson color. It brought to mind jam on sticky fingers and kisses under an old oak tree. It was tied at the top with an unassuming bit of twine. The lovely fragrance of cloves and something earthy filled the air as he held it out to her.

All at once, her mood soured. Something shimmered in the air around them and an unreasonable yet undeniable sense of dread filled her as she looked at the bundle.

"What is it?"

"A gift."

His smile was reassuring, but she couldn't help the words that tumbled from her lips. "I don't want it."

His smile fell.

"You think I wish harm to fall on you." It wasn't a question. In that uncanny way of his, he'd read her mood to perfection.

"No. Never."

"Then why so quickly refuse my token?"

She didn't want to refuse him anything, but something in her was ill at ease. "Tell me what it is."

"A simple charm."

"From your mother?"

He nodded.

"Why?"

"It's for you but not for you. A token of my affection for you and all that you are. All those you hold dear."

"What does that mean?" she asked.

"Affection? I thought we understood one another." He cocked his head in that birdlike way.

"I know what affection is. What does it mean it's for me but not for me?"

"It's for your father. Or more precisely, Elwell & Sons."

"It's a gift for the carnival itself?"

He nodded. How could a gift be for the carnival?

Again he read her expression as easily as if she'd spoken her feelings aloud. "It's a simple charm to bring about ongoing prosperity, vitality, and endurance. I'd hoped it would ease your worry. About those you hold close to your heart."

He was giving her the gift of freedom from her father's debts. If the charm worked and the carnival thrived, she'd have no reason to stay and see after things. Maybe it was her own fear of letting go that had prompted her reaction to the small sachet.

"Oh. That's very thoughtful."

His face was grim and expectant as if he wanted her to take it but also worried that she would.

"I feel like there's something you aren't telling me," she said.

"I have few secrets. And those I'd share if you ask."

"So I'll ask them. Why don't you want me to take this?"

"I want very much for you to take it. But it did come at a price." If there was ever a time for him to speak plainly, it was now.

"What price?"

"Something I didn't realize I cared about, until I met you."

"More riddles." She tried to keep the frustration out of her voice.

"One day I'll share the answer with you. This I swear."

He tugged again on a lock of her hair, running it between his fingers. His eyes watched her, and she felt lighter somehow. Not at all worried about all the questions she'd had just hours before.

"Will you now accept it? On behalf of the carnival?"

She grimaced an apology. "Yes. Of course."

The moment the cloth hit her palm, the smell of fire and salt filled her nose. She was suddenly nauseous.

"You should have let me explain what affection means. I would have stumbled and made myself a fool. I'm sure it would have been quite entertaining."

She felt the color draining from her face and stumbled. "Making a fool of you is not my idea of entertainment." She was going to be sick.

Was this the price he meant?

"Sweetling?" There was an urgency in his voice, and she knew immediately if this was the sachet's doing, he'd had no inkling it would.

He helped her to sit on the damp grass. With one hand he brushed sweat-soaked locks of her honey blonde hair from her face. "You are unwell. What can I do?"

"It's been a long day. I just need a moment."

There's been some trouble. It was when the wind came through and the lamps went out. Why don't you ask your friend?

Just because he didn't know the effect the charm might have on her didn't mean he hadn't played a part in the earlier unpleasantness.

Her voice was reedy as she asked, "Where did you say you were earlier this evening?"

"With my brothers. Coming back from my mother's newest abode."

Evil and Violence. Had they been the ones to rile the crowd just as Darkness blew out the lamps?

It couldn't be. What reason would they have for it?

"Sweetling?"

"You're right. I don't feel well." She ran a shaking hand over her hair. "Maybe it has to do with what happened earlier."

He didn't look convinced. He kept his gaze on the sachet in her hand, his brow furrowed. It was the darkest she'd ever seen him. "Mayhap."

"There was some trouble earlier tonight." She hated using the words her father and CJ had but didn't know how else to put it. "Some men turned violent. One of the troupe was badly beaten."

"That's dire news. I'm sorry for your people." He still looked distracted. Distracted and even a bit scared.

"It happened when the lamps went out."

He finally looked up at her, his frown deepening. "Ah. I see. Violence following darkness."

"It wasn't . . . I mean, you and your brother weren't. . ." She couldn't finish the sentence. Couldn't voice what she'd been so worried about.

"No, Bronwen. We didn't bring our trouble to your door. I thought . . . well, never mind what I thought."

Guilt and shame left a bitter taste in her mouth. This was Darkness. Her Darkness.

"Are you well enough to walk now?"

She nodded, and he helped her to her feet.

"I don't think I can work the confections wagon. Do you mind just taking me to my accommodation?"

"I'll do anything you ask of me."

"Will you stay for a bit? There's something not right. I don't know what it is, but I'd appreciate the company."

He held her elbow, and she felt the tiny flutter in her stomach she always got when he touched her.

When they reached the wagon she shared with Enid, they sat on the steps and waited in a warm silence. He kissed her once. It was sweet and gentle and full of the promise of so many things to come. It made her forget her earlier concerns, the doubt Enid had raised, and the possibility that he was anything but the man she wanted to run away with.

If Bronwen had known it was the last good night they would be together, she would have opened her soul to him. Would have shared all the longing and love she had for him in her heart. But she didn't know what was waiting for them just hours away, and so she loved him quietly and privately.

The next day, after everything that was revealed in the

following hours, she swore she would always remember that quiet time they'd shared. The way he held her hand. The way he tasted when he kissed her softly. The way he wrapped the strands of her hair around his fingers. The way he smelled and the way he moved. She vowed to herself that she would always remember how fiercely she loved him.

She didn't know how wrong she was.

Twenty-eight

BEFORE

"That can't be. Da, tell me that can't be."

Bronwen had turned away from CJ and stood facing her father, only inches from his downturned face. Alfie Elwell didn't speak.

Bronwen spun back toward CJ, trying to change the words she had just heard falling from his lips.

Your father wagered the carnival. Wagered and lost.

"I know it's not pleasant to hear, but think how much worse it'd be if it was to someone other than me." CJ was trying to sound reassuring but was failing miserably. She didn't care who her father had lost it to. He'd lost it and that was all that mattered. "That crack Sheffly. He'd have half the troupe gone in days and the other half would spend all their time on broken attractions and in worn-out costumes. This way things will remain *mostly* unchanged."

It was the *mostly* that gutted her. He couldn't possibly believe she should be happy that her father had lost everything to him. That she should be thankful he'd been the one to upend her entire life.

Not just her life, but Enid's too.

"So we work for you now?" Enid asked, unbelieving.

"In and off as much as you worked for your da," CJ said. "Yeah."

"But you aren't our da."

"No, but I'm like family, right?"

Enid didn't understand her next words would hit CJ like the blow they were, but Bronwen saw his face morph the moment her sister said them. "Like isn't the same as is."

"Well. I guess you'll all just have to get used to it, won't you?" His tone turned petulant.

Finally her father spoke. "Now, girls. Let's not worry too much, aye. Elwell & Sons will persevere. We always do."

"Well, now. I've been thinking about that actually," CJ said. "It won't be Elwell much longer, will it? I'll need to find a printer and get the lads to repaint the bigger signage."

"You're changing the name?" Bronwen was incredulous. "It's always been Elwell."

"Well, as dear Enid just pointed out, I'm not family, am I? It only makes sense to update things accordingly."

She looked to her father and watched as a single tear trailed down the line of his cheek and dangled at his chin before splashing to the front of his cravat.

"You girls can keep your wagon obviously and keep your spots in the troupe. In fact, I'm not sure what I'd do if you left." CJ gave a nervous laugh.

Keep their wagon? Of course they would keep their wagon. It was *their* wagon. Their home.

"Alfie, I'm sure we can find something for you, too. You've got such a great voice after all. Always know how to draw in the crowds."

He was talking as if their world wasn't crashing down all around them. Bronwen couldn't stand it.

"At any rate. You should all get some sleep." As if she could sleep. CJ looked at the sisters and dusted off his hands. "I'll be talking to the troupe in the morning, and then we head out. I have big plans. Big, big plans."

CJ left them. Her father didn't speak. Just kissed them each on the cheek and drifted off to be alone with his shame.

Bronwen looked around for someone to tell her it was all a joke. Just a mean-spirited jest. No one was there.

"This can't be happening," Bronwen said to no one in particular. How could things have gone this far?

"Well, that does it then," Enid said.

"Does what?"

"Gives you what you want."

"What I want? Did Clive drop you on your head? In what world would this be what I want?" Her words were rushed and verging on tears.

"In the world where you get to run off and leave me behind." Enid's words were full of venom. Bronwen was momentarily stunned.

"Enid." Bronwen's voice quavered. She took a deep breath. "I've never wanted to leave you behind. I always assumed it would be you leaving. For bigger and better things. I suppose now you've got that chance."

She scoffed. "You can't think I'd leave now?"

"Why not? We could go together." As soon as she said it, she knew it was the best option. They could take what money they had and leave. Between the two of them, they could make a fresh start. "We can get set up in the city. Just as you've always talked about. Get jobs." She could still have a life with Darkness. She'd still see him every night, and then once Enid was doing well on her own, she would be free to live her life with him. Maybe this wasn't as bad as she'd first thought.

Enid shook her head, eyes wide and disbelieving. "All this time, Winnie, I thought you understood. I mean something to this troupe. I am someone. CJ knows that. I can't leave. This carnival needs me."

"But it's not ours anymore. This is your chance."

"What does it matter whose name is on the ticket stubs?"

"So you're staying. And working for CJ?"

Enid nodded. "The show still needs you too, Winnie. It'd be selfish for you to leave now. The troupe respects you."

"The show doesn't need me. Not anymore."

"Well, I do. More than that, Da needs you. If you go, the others will follow. Then what happens?" She was angry. Bronwen couldn't fathom it. Of all the people in this debacle, her sister was angry at Bronwen. For daring to want something else for herself.

"I can't."

"You can." Enid stepped forward and grasped both of Bronwen's hands. "You barely know him. In time, he'll forget all about you, but we won't, Winnie. If he was normal or plain, I'd understand. But you can't honestly tell me you'd rather chase after a man you know so little about. I said it before. He will watch you age and then he will get bored of you and he will leave. And during that time, what do you suppose will become of us?"

"You don't know him, Enid." Her voice was barely above a whisper.

"And really neither do you." Enid pulled Bronwen into a fierce hug and whispered in her ear, "Please, Winnie. Please stay here, with me. If it's only for a short time, fine. But you can't leave now. You just can't. We need you."

Enid stood before her, tears in her eyes, and Bronwen felt herself torn in two. Torn between who she wanted and who she was.

Enid might have been right about some things, but she was oh so very wrong about the rest. Bronwen did know Darkness. She knew him like she knew her own face. She knew him like she knew sugar, and he knew her like he knew shadows.

It was because he loved her that he would let her go if she asked.

And she loved him. Completely and without question. Her doubts in him were gone. He was the one person in this world she could rely on. It broke her. Right down the center. A deep throbbing pain she could only hope would eventually turn numb.

She loved him. She always would. Him and no one else.

She turned and bolted for the only place she wanted to be in that exact moment—into the arms of Darkness.

He waited for her just inside the tree line, arms open. Bronwen stumbled into him with the force of her grief.

He didn't speak. Didn't call her sweetling. Didn't ask what troubled her. He simply held her while she wept.

When at last her tears stopped flowing, she felt empty and hollow. Every happy thought she'd ever held had abandoned her. Every bit of joy she'd spread meant nothing. Every breath and heartbeat and fiber of her was about to be changed forever.

But she couldn't continue to tie him to her here. He deserved better. He deserved to move with the wind and the night. He deserved a life where he wouldn't need to choose between serving his purpose and following the carnival from stop to stop.

It simply never occurred to her that he might not mind the traveling. That he might want to follow wherever the circuit took her. That he might have a choice in this as well.

She was a hollow husk when she finally spoke. "You once told me you would do anything for me. Anything I asked. No questions, no arguments. Do you remember that?" She couldn't look at him.

Not now.

She wanted to remember his beautiful face as it currently sat in her mind. The quizzical expressions and slightest smiles. The depth of his black eyes when he looked at her as if she were the most cherished thing in all the world.

If she looked at him now, she would only remember the pain and sorrow and confusion she was sure to see.

"Sweetling? Look at me."

She shook her head and stared at her feet.

Her voice was thick as she choked down the sob she knew was waiting to come. "I am asking you now to do something for me. No questions and no arguments."

"Look at me, Bronwen."

"I can't." She gagged on the words.

"You can. Look at me. Please."

"I need you to leave, Darkness. I can't have this." She moved her hands back and forth between them. "Your shadows. Your power. Your family. Leave tonight and never look back. Don't return to the carnival. Don't leave me—" Her voice broke and she choked. "Don't leave me another stone. Don't hide in the shadows. Leave me and live your fantastical magical life without me in it."

"You can't ask that. You can't."

"I can. I am." The tears were streaming down her face.

"When I made that promise, I never thought. . ." He sounded as broken as she felt, and she hated herself for doing that to him. He deserved so much better.

She hoped one day he would find it. He had a long life ahead of him after all.

"But you did promise. No questions, remember."

He made a broken sound, and she thought if she stood there a moment longer, she might die from the pain of it.

"Goodbye, Darkness."

And then she fled. Like the coward she was.

She never looked up. Never saw how long he stood staring after her. Never let herself love anyone again.

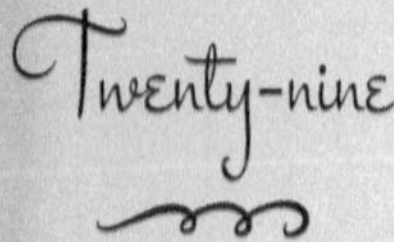

Twenty-nine

"I stayed." Bronwen was shocked by the memory. Shocked by her own foolishness and her sister's manipulation. That she'd allowed herself to be manipulated into doing something so unthinkable. "He wanted me to leave with him and I stayed. For you." Her voice sounded just as hollow as she felt. It was the same hollowness from all those years ago, just as fresh as ever.

Perhaps losing her memory had been a blessing after all.

Enid sat up straighter but didn't rise to approach Bronwen where she stood. It was probably for the best. She wasn't certain how she would react if Enid got too close.

"You stayed for *us*, Winnie. It wasn't just me. You were doubting him and I could see that."

"It wasn't for me. He loved me." She made no attempt to stop the tears sliding down her cheeks. He deserved the tears. Even if she didn't.

No wonder he couldn't trust her now. She couldn't even trust herself.

"He didn't even fight for you." Enid's voice was just this side of cruel. "He never came back. What kind of love is that?"

"The best kind. I asked him to leave and he did. He didn't make me beg, didn't make it any harder for me than it had to be. And for what? This?"

The memory of that night sat like molten sugar in her belly. Hot and burning and nauseatingly sweet.

She remembered the rest now too. How things had changed after CJ took over. Him insisting they were like family but treating her father like dirt. Enid gradually siding with him more and more, until one day her father withered away and Bronwen could do nothing to pull him back from it. Enid mourning but not really. Always pushing for bigger and brighter and gawdier. The underlying understanding that CJ wanted more from Enid than she would ever give but still bowing to her whims more often than not. In their own twisted ways, they deserved each other.

And Bronwen realized she deserved them too.

She'd had the greatest of all things, the love of Darkness. And it took only a few well-chosen words from her sister for Bronwen to be persuaded to throw it all away. She was no better than either of them.

Then there was the carousel. Enid hadn't been lying when she said Bronwen had fought it. Not after the first time she saw what it could truly do.

They'd been traveling under CJ's name for several years the first time the thing showed its true power. Bronwen had been unsettled by it from the day she'd sent Darkness away, but she'd always chalked it up to the general melancholy she felt knowing her one true happiness had been destroyed by her own hand. Each and every time she got near the spinning horses, she felt slightly ill—a wave of nausea or an unexpected headache. But the crowds loved it. They lined up two or three deep to have a go.

Things hadn't been going particularly well for the troupe for a number of years. The core of them were still the same, but they were having trouble attracting fresh talent. CJ was prickly and the general air of the place felt stale.

They'd been camped in a particularly tough little town set low against the mountains. The folk there were miners mostly and more than a little rough around the edges. Kerb was getting slower and crankier by the day, as was CJ. Alfie Elwell had already passed, and several of the troupe had been dealing with one particularly unsavory man who just wouldn't let up on any of the performers. He chucked insults and bottles and was escorted out of one tent after another just to barge straight into the next.

Bronwen hadn't been there to witness what happened that night, but she got a detailed account from more than one member of the troupe, Enid included.

They had been closing up, ready to pack the wagons for the next day. The man had seated himself on one of the spring horses and was refusing to leave. Kerb, having had enough, got a few of the fellas, and they ran that ride back and forth a dozen times, each getting progressively faster than the last. At first, the man laughed and called for more, but about six rides in he began to scream for them to stop. The screaming turned to crying. The crying to begging. Finally, he fell silent. Eventually the mechanism caught and stuck halfway up the pole. Sensing his chance, he jumped down, landing in the hay piled up underneath. He'd gone from a hale man in his twenties to aged and withered, barely able to walk himself out of the show.

CJ, having witnessed the whole thing, and more than curious about anything that might make a bigger name for himself or revitalize the show, climbed up the ride and reset the tethers, then rode it to the ground. He was the only one not completely astonished when he climbed off looking and feeling ten years younger.

His transformation had been subtle enough that it could be hidden from some of the troupe. The first time at least.

Over the course of the next two decades, either his understanding of the process or the magic itself grew stronger, until eventually he could turn back the clock quite alarmingly. CJ had never been a dull man, and he knew he needed to keep a tight leash on things. He and Kerb and Enid put together a roster of which troupe members to let in on the secret. And they got more than proficient at swapping out the others, hiring and firing and rebuilding over the span of a month or two.

After that first vile night, when CJ tapped into the magic, things turned around for the troupe. Even with the downtime, the carnival was always a success. They never had to want for patrons. Never had to worry about not feeding the performers. They could take on new acts and almost overnight they would be a success, drawing in crowds upon crowds. CJ had drive and ambition, and the carnival never let him down.

If only it had been like that for her father. Instead Alfie had died a sad and broken man.

Bronwen refused to stay and be a party to it any longer.

She touched the pile of stones by her bed. Knowing she couldn't take them all, she picked up a pair of them—the first and the last ones she'd gotten from Darkness—along with the small sachet that had always rested beside them, and placed the items in her pocket. They were to serve as reminders of all she had lost.

"Goodbye, Enid." She smiled sadly at her sister.

"It's easy for you. You can get along anywhere. Make your little candies anywhere, until the day you die. But what about me, Winnie?" Enid's voice shook as she spoke. "What am I to do once my face is lined and my bones no longer allow me to be who I am?"

Now it was Bronwen's turn to pity her sister. "Then you

do what everyone does. You try to be a decent person and you find something else to make you happy."

Enid looked back at her in confused disbelief.

It had taken lifetimes, but Bronwen was finally able to leave her sister behind.

✳

Darkness was likely long gone. The water maiden was safely out of the camp, and there was no reason for him to linger.

A small part of her hoped he could leave and not look back. He deserved that much. To be free from even the memory of her.

She had no idea what she could say to him at this point. Words seemed insufficient. *Sorry I didn't love you fiercely enough?*

If there was any fairness in the world, he would have moved on quickly. And perhaps he had. He'd been able to forget her for decades after all.

The troupe hadn't settled for the night just yet. Lights still twinkled here and there. The smell of woodsmoke and sausages lingered. Laughter bubbled from this stall or that. It was normal except for the occasional shouts of voices belonging to Kerb, CJ, and a few others. She didn't think Enid would rat her out to them, but she'd rather not find out exactly where her sister's loyalties actually lay.

She stuck to the edges of the camp, heading for the side. She slipped under the ropes and down the narrow lane that led to the village of Feyport. She could taste freedom and the unknown.

Then she heard the haunting tinkle of the carousel music pick up and she froze.

If the water maiden had escaped, why would CJ need the carousel to run?

Because he was dying. She'd seen how frail he'd become. Seen the blood on his handkerchief.

Even if he didn't have a fey creature to charge the hideous magic, he didn't need one. Not really. He could do what he'd done scores of times before. Charge it with a drunk or a miscreant or any one of a pile of men he'd deemed worthy of the ride.

She was six kinds of fool to have thought any differently. She had to stop it but didn't know how. Perhaps if Darkness or one of his brothers was still nearby, they might lend assistance. Even the dashing selkie seemed willing to help. But thinking of him made her think of Enid, and that way lay nothing but more heartache.

It didn't really matter. There was no time for fetching them.

Without thinking a drop more about it, she turned and raced back into the camp and straight for the carousel.

Thirty

The sight that greeted her was so much worse than she could have imagined.

The ride was running, albeit at a rather slow pace. Nightmare creatures crawled after one another in an insidious never-ending race. The music was playing and the lights were flashing.

And riding on its slow circles were CJ and Kerb. Enid was at the ride's gate, her back to Bronwen. She must have left the wagon just after Bronwen had. Tears left tracks through her makeup, though her eyes were dry now.

CJ looked as if he might fall, there on the spot. His skin was wan and waxy, his beard patchy, hair thinned to the point where she could see a smattering of age spots on his scalp. He was hunched and bent and nearly broken.

Kerb looked uneasy.

It didn't take much to see why.

A boy stood between CJ and Kerb, hands tied behind his back. His feet were planted to help maintain balance as the creatures around him slowly bobbed up and down. His face was drained of color, making the scar on his brow stand out in sharp relief. As Bronwen approached, he looked at her with wide terrified eyes.

Tommy.

"What's going on here?" Bronwen pushed past her sister and climbed up onto the slow-moving attraction. "Tommy, let's go."

She tried to nudge him to run, but he shook his head, staying put.

"Oh, how lovely," CJ croaked, followed by a short barking cough. This time not just flecks but gobs of blood flew from between his lips. He wiped at his mouth with the sleeve of his jacket. "Kerb?" He nodded at Tommy.

"This doesn't seem right, boss. He's one of us."

"I don't give two turds what seems right." CJ drew a deep rattling breath.

"Tommy, go on now," Bronwen urged. "He won't hurt me."

Again Tommy shook his head.

"You seem awfully sure of that, considering it's likely down to you we're all here now," CJ said.

"CJ. It's time to end this. Please."

"Time. It's a fickle thing, is it not," CJ mused then relented. "Kerb, take him. I'd like a moment alone with Bronwen."

Kerb reluctantly moved to grab Tommy, but the boy pushed him back.

"Go on, now. Stand over there with Enid. I'll be fine." It was only after this Tommy relented and let Kerb usher him off the ride.

Relieved he was off the thing, Bronwen could finally breathe. Hands in her pockets, Bronwen dropped onto a bench carved to resemble a pair of pookas holding up the long narrow seat.

Enid's eyes went wide, and she shook her head. Bronwen smiled at her sadly.

Tommy too must have sensed something in her posture, for he immediately tried to climb up beside her. Kerb grabbed him and held him in place, seeming unsure what to do.

On the next revolution, she tilted her head to the open seat beside her and looked at CJ. "Come on. One last ride for old time's sake."

CJ chuckled and shook his head, holding himself up against the terrible kelpie. "Last ride, hmm? Sounds as if you know something I do not."

"Just the opposite." She smiled bitterly. "I don't think I know much of anything at all."

The ride continued. Now Enid, Kerb, and Tommy were in sight. Now they were not. Round and round and round.

When another revolution completed, he smiled at her. Blood stained his teeth.

"Come down from there, Winnie," Enid called.

Bronwen was done letting Enid talk her into things. "I think it's my turn. To ride it forward. It's been my turn for quite a while, don't you think?"

Finally releasing the vicious water horse, CJ still refused to sit. He walked against the rotation, slow shuffling steps that kept him even with the others who stood on solid ground.

Slowly rotating. Again on the far side. She dug into her pocket and pulled out the sachet.

This time, when she came around, she held it up. "How about you come have a seat, CJ, or I destroy this."

CJ wore a bemused expression. "A trinket to keep your knickers smelling fresh? Be my guest."

Bronwen had traveled to the far side of the carousel so didn't see when the others approached. She wasn't sure if she should be terrified or elated when she heard the smoky silk of Carman's voice when she said, "Oh, dearest. If you think that, you really should reconsider your position in the world."

On the next revolution she couldn't help the melting feeling that blossomed in her chest. Darkness stood beside his mother, watching as CJ looked utterly baffled by the woman.

"All this time and you thought what? You just stumbled upon some little spell or enchantment?" Carman asked.

CJ and Kerb both looked befuddled, but Enid didn't; she looked like every dream she had ever had was about to be crushed under the weight of the witch's stare.

The ride continued to rotate, taking Bronwen away from the unfolding drama just to circle her right back to it.

"That, dearest, is mine." Carman's tone had lost its silk and sweetness. Now it was vengeance and fury and retribution. "My magic. My charm. My doing. Corrupted into this." She pointed at the slowly turning monstrosity.

A weight was lifted from Bronwen's chest. She'd been right.

It was the gift from Carman, bestowed on the carnival all those years ago, that had led to this darkness. If she could destroy it somehow, maybe this evil would end.

"Yours?" CJ cried. "I have built this place from almost nothing. I'll not let anyone say otherwise."

"It was never meant for you, you fool. When you greedily took what didn't belong to you, the charm didn't know how to behave," Carman said. "It bent just as you bent. It darkened just as you darkened."

Bronwen's relief at having the answer was short-lived. "This too was my fault."

"Yes. In a way." Carman was angry, and Bronwen couldn't blame her.

"Mother." There was a warning in Darkness's tone.

"And no," Carman relented. "It was something I overlooked. I simply didn't expect things to develop as they did."

Darkness looked at Bronwen, concern and anger etched into every line of his being. "Bronwen, come down from there." She frowned. "Now. Please."

"I can't. I'm sorry. For all of it. Dub"—she watched as he squeezed his eyes shut at the sound of his name on her lips—"this needs to end."

"It will. The bauble. Give Mother the bauble." His tone was firm and sure.

Could that really work? If she gave the charm back, would that be the end? Surely it couldn't be so simple. But what did she know of magic or charms? Her only spellwork was with sugar and spice. Unless you counted the unwilling theft of years.

She squeezed the sachet and looked to Darkness. "All right." She stood to climb down.

"No," CJ said. "Give me the charm, Bronwen."

No one stopped her. Tommy might have tried, had Kerb not still held his arm. Not Enid who looked as if she couldn't decide if she wanted her to succeed or not. Not Darkness or Carman who clearly weren't expecting what came next.

They all just watched as Bronwen rose from the bench. She looked directly at Darkness. "I'm sorry I didn't remember that you loved me. And I'm sorry I was too weak to let you do it properly from the first." Then grabbing tight to the nearest pole with one arm, she reached down with the other and pushed the carousel's controller lever to high.

Bronwen wasn't certain what she'd hoped to achieve. Not really.

Having made it back to his starting spot, CJ stumbled as the ride picked up speed and fell forward into the garish face of the nightmare kelpie. He clung to it as if it were alive and taking him to the depths of the sea.

Bronwen thought to jump off the ride and moved to the edge. But then CJ was moving and yelling to Kerb. "Stop the ride. Reverse it."

And she couldn't have that. Not again. Not taking all of those years that belonged to someone else. Better to stay here and make sure it ended. It was a fair and worthy price.

She only needed to make sure CJ was on the ride with her.

She grabbed on and wrapped her arms tight around him.

"The charm, lovely. Throw me the charm." Carman yelling.

"Stop the ride." CJ screaming.

He was growing older moment by moment. She supposed she was too. But he'd been frail when they'd gotten on this thing and she had been full of vitality. She had more rotations in her than he did.

She didn't want to know how bad it would get, but she couldn't tear her eyes away.

Deeper wrinkles formed. His skin grew tight over his cheeks. His eyes began to run.

He still had some fight in him though. The man she once thought of as a brother pawed at her, and she lost her balance, falling back and hitting her head on the tarnished pole behind her.

She was dazed but still she managed to toss the charm. It had to be the right direction, didn't it? The lights were flashing by and the music was fading in and out and she was going to be sick.

And then Darkness was there and he was pulling her close and then pushing her away and then she was tumbling through space and maybe even through time and it was dark and then light and then dark again, but she liked the darkness because without darkness she couldn't be anyone's light and she smiled as she fell.

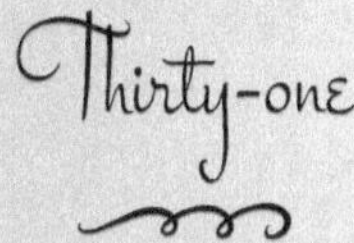

Thirty-one

"**S**weetling."

Bronwen was dreaming. In it she was walking through brightly colored carnival lights. Red and blue and golden. Merry music bubbled and the air was filled with burnt sugar and honeysuckle. Darkness was there, kissing her neck and promising a future she would never have.

"Open your eyes, Sweetling."

The dream began to dissolve, replaced by the nightmare she knew to be true. Lives lived on stolen years.

"Come now, Sweetling."

"You should give her a moment, Dub. It was quite a tumble."

Her head was pounding and her shoulder was screaming.

"Come now, Sweetling. Open those eyes."

She groaned.

"That's my good girl."

A snort. "Perhaps you're the one who hit your head. All those years pining for someone who threw it all away."

"Not now."

"Does she even know the price you paid?"

Here it was. The nightmare. She couldn't face him.

"Sweetling." His voice rose at the end. Another warning. This time gentle and just for her.

Warm arms held her tenderly.

She cracked her eyes open. All she could see was Darkness. Dark eyes. Dark hair. Dark expression.

With a trembling hand, she felt the lump rising on her forehead and winced for her effort.

"We'll get that looked at."

"We?"

He nodded.

The lights from the carousel were still burning brightly, but the music had stopped. It was almost eerily quiet.

She tried to sit up and winced again. He helped her.

Standing just behind him were Carman and Tommy. The witch was speaking softly to the young man. Bronwen wondered if she should be concerned, but Tommy just looked at the beautiful woman with wide eyes. There was the barest trace of a smile on his face.

"How bad is it?" Darkness asked.

"I'll not be pulling taffy for a spell. That's certain." She looked back to the carousel. "CJ?"

"It was time his payment came due."

She nodded, and though she wanted to feel nothing but relief, she found the tiniest bit of sadness as well. They'd grown up together after all. Despite his many faults, they had lived countless lives and adventures together. Even if those years weren't of her choosing.

"Before you ask, Enid and her friend are fine. They've gone with Declan. He had some questions."

"Declan?"

"The selkie, lovely. He's what happens when folks misbehave here in Feyport," Carman explained. Done talking with Tommy, she looked down on Bronwen and Darkness. "I'll leave you to it then. And I'll be taking this with me." She held up the sachet, faded and brittle now, its magic all used up.

Bronwen understood that Declan had been the man sent with Violence to rescue Neeve. She worried what he would make of Kerb and Enid. Of her.

"It's not just the two of them. There were others. I—"

"Not now. He'll want to speak with you, true. But not now."

She swallowed and nodded.

"Did you mean it, Sweetling?"

"Mean what?"

"What you said. At the last? Are you sorry?"

"More than I could ever say."

He rolled his lower lip between his teeth and looked away toward the trees. He seemed to come to a decision of sorts and nodded.

"Right then. Let's get you up." He helped her stand. "To your wagon then." He looked to Tommy, uncertainty shadowing his expression.

"Whatever you need, you can trust him," Bronwen said.

"All right." Speaking to Tommy, he said, "Head to the village, if you would. Fetch whoever passes as a healer there and bring them back."

Tommy nodded and, without a second thought, did as he was asked.

Darkness held her uninjured arm as they walked back toward her wagon.

"You called me sweetling. When I was waking. You haven't called me that in a very long time."

"You aren't mistaken. I didn't think you wanted me to."

"I understand if you despise me. I despise myself."

"I don't despise you."

"How can you not?"

"You did what you thought others needed. I cannot fault you for it."

"I can fault myself enough for both of us."

"I should have come back. Should never have upheld that promise. I was just as much a fool as you," he said. "I thought about it. Every day. Until I was going mad with it. I wasn't my best self in those years after."

"I'm sorry I did that to you."

"We have a lot to atone for. Both of us, I believe."

She nodded. "What was the price, Darkness?"

"What price?"

"Carman. Your mother, she said I didn't even know the price. Was it for the charm all those years ago."

"Indeed." He grimaced.

"And what was it?" She wasn't certain she wanted to know but needed to ask.

He sighed and rubbed a hand over his brow. "When I asked her for the charm to save the carnival for you, I had to pay with something."

"What was the price, Darkness?"

"It seemed more important to her than to me. More important to my brothers. I'd never really valued it and there was something I wanted more. I wanted your happiness. For your father to prosper. For you to feel as if you could finally leave."

"What price?" She was urgent now.

"My immortality. I traded my immortality. I thought . . . I thought we could grow old together. To live a full life together."

Her heart broke all over again. She hadn't just been a fool and a coward, she'd been selfish and arrogant. She hadn't even given him a chance to explain. Just asked that he leave, and he'd done it.

"But you're still here. If you traded your immortality, how are you still here?"

"That part of the charm was broken when you sent me away. Just as the magic morphed to be ugly and dark, so too did it release me from my payment."

"That's why she thanked me? Because you were immortal still?"

He nodded. "And I could stay with her and my brothers. They didn't lose me after all."

"Oh. But now." Bronwen closed her eyes. She couldn't look at him. Everything he'd done for her and she'd foolishly dared to hope for just the smallest moment that she might find a sliver of happiness after all of it.

"But now." He paused.

They'd made it back to her wagon.

And she was right back to where she'd been before. She was young once more, but he was immortal. She would grow old now and finally meet her rest. He would not.

But then it clicked. She found she didn't really care.

If she could be with him for just another day, a week, a year, she would leap to it. Leap forward to the unknown. The adventure. But as Violence had said just hours ago, that crow had called.

"It's odd," he said. "How I feel no different."

She frowned. "What do you mean?"

"The carousel. I had to ride it through til the end. To ensure your friend's price was paid in full. And at long last to pay mine as well, I suppose. I assumed I'd feel different."

"Your price?" The sweet selfish part of her reared up again. Could he really mean it?

"The charm demanded it. I'd been living under a debt myself. Now it has been satisfied."

Bronwen stumbled at the steps. "So you'll be. . ." She couldn't think how to phrase it.

He didn't make her suffer. "We have much to catch up on, Sweetling."

"I don't think I'm the same person I was," she said quietly.

"Nor am I. Would you care to get to know me again?" He held out his hand to her, palm clenched.

She turned it over and pulled his fingers open, revealing a small moss-colored stone.

"What will it cost me?" she asked.

He leaned forward and brushed his lips against hers in the faintest blush of a kiss. "I hear you make the most magical bonbons. I'd like one of those to start."

Here I am at the end of another Simple Tales book. And here you are, having made it to the end with me. I truly hope you enjoyed it at least a little.

I want to say this book almost wrote itself, but that isn't actually quite right. It wanted to write itself, but my life got in the way of its plans. That sounds kooky, I realize. Let me explain.

If you've read the other Simple Tales books, you know Darkness made his first appearance in A Simple Tale of Ink and Bindings. While I adore Fia and Tieg, the moment I put Carman and her son Darkness on the page, I couldn't stop thinking about him. The original story of Carman and her sons comes from old Irish folklore. In the original tales, Carman was an evil sorceress from Athens who, with the aid of her equally terrible sons, invaded Ireland and brought a blight of disease and famine to the land. She was eventually defeated and imprisoned and her sons were banished back across the sea.

Like quite a bit of my writing, I took quite a bit of liberty with the characters, and really grew fond of them by the end of the process. I knew before I'd even finished Ink and Bindings, that I wanted to do more with them and with Darkness in particular.

Almost as soon as I decided to give Dub his own story, I knew exactly what I wanted it to be.

As a kid, I loved all things slightly creepy and one of my favorite films from my childhood was the Jason Robards and

Jonathan Pryce beauty, *Something Wicked This Way Comes*. It wasn't until much later that I realized it was a classic Ray Bradbury novel, which it turns out, I loved just as much. The story of Darkness just had to take place in a dark carnival. But how to make it a cozy romance? The answer came almost just as quickly. Make it a play on my favorite Jane Austen story, *Persuasion*.

It was all set in my head. I could see exactly how it would play out. I should be able to sit down and bang it out in a matter of weeks. I was so excited.

And then we decided to move. Not across the street, or even across town. No. We were going to fulfill a dream and move to the Pacific Northwest. Add in my actual real-life job and the world being a mess, and being a halfway decent mother and wife, and time for writing, grew almost non-existent. So, the book sat in my head and in some scratched lines in my notebook and it took me so much longer to find time to get to it than I would have liked. But when I finally did, I fell in love with the whole thing all over again.

Finishing it was a treat and it's given me the drive I needed to finally finish telling the story I started so many years ago—Aylee and Cailean's story. Look for the final Simple Tales book sometime in the next year.

As always, I want to thank my amazing copy and line editor Karen Robinson. As always, I vow to one day learn the proper placement of a comma! I also need to thank my beautiful family for supporting all of my crazy dreams. I couldn't do any of this without you. And to you the readers who have made it this far, thanks are just not enough. These stories don't mean anything if no one reads them. I'd offer you a cherry lime bonbon if I could.

About the Author

Kami King Larsen is a native of the Desert Southwest, US. She recently followed a troupe of faeries to the land of mushrooms and snails and now calls the Pacific Northwest home. She is a practicing pediatrician by training and a lover of great stories and all things whimsical by birth. Kami writes cozy fantasy romance and science fantasy fiction.

Let's Connect

If you are interested in the opportunity to receive free Advanced Reader Copies for future releases and keep up with other exciting news, head over to my website https://www.kamikinglarsenbooks.com , join my mailing list, or follow me on social media!

Thank you for taking the time to share in Darkness and Bronwen's story. The best way to support authors is to leave a review on Amazon, Goodreads, you social media channels, or anywhere else you review books.